The
D(

Millennium Edition

Edited by

Derrick Belanger, PSI

Belanger Books

Print and Digital Edition The Pontine Dossier Millennium Edition Vol. 1 No. 1© 2019 by Belanger Books, LLC

ISBN: 9781679930386

All Rights Reserved. No part of this book may be used or reproduced in any manner whatsoever without written permission except in case of brief quotations embodied in critical articles or reviews.

Submissions to The Pontine Dossier should be sent by email to derrick@belangerbooks.com

For information contact:

Belanger Books, LLC

61 Theresa Ct.

Manchester, NH 03103

derrick@belangerbooks.com

www.belangerbooks.com

Cover, Internal Artwork, and Back Cover design by Brian Belanger

https://www.redbubble.com/people/zhahadun

https://zhahadun.wixsite.com/221b

Table of Contents

Solar Pons Scholarship for the 21st Century by Derrick Belanger, PSI and Brian Belanger, PSI 5

The World of August Derleth: Capturing the Spirit of Wisconsin Through Literature by Chris Chan 7

But Was She a Vampire? by Derrick Belanger, PSI 27

How Deep Did the Amworthy Hoax Go? by James C. O'Leary, PSI 33

"The Name is Pons... *Solar* Pons!" by Robert Pohle, PSI 52

Did Solar Pons Really Meet Hercule Poirot on the Orient Express? by Chris Chan 59

The Long Return of Solar Pons by David Marcum, PSI
.... 64

To Pastiche or not to Pastiche by Stephen Herczeg ... 78

Solar Pons Scholarship for the 21st Century
An Introduction to the Millennium edition of the Pontine Dossier

By Derrick Belanger, PSI and Brian Belanger, PSI

In January 2019 at the BSI weekend in New York, we had the honor of meeting longtime Ponsian writer and publisher George A. Vanderburgh. He was a friendly man, eloquent in his speech, and a passionate admirer of Solar Pons. As most of you know, Mr. Vanderburgh published a number of Solar Pons collections through his company The Battered Silicon Dispatch Box, including the beautiful two-volume Solar Pons Omnibus.

We hit it off and spent much of our time together discussing the new Solar Pons collections by Belanger Books, the PSI (we received our investiture from Mr. Vanderburgh shortly thereafter), and the possibility of more Pontine scholarship.

Vanderburgh had the brilliant idea of publishing a brand-new edition of the Pontine Dossier, that Solar Pons publication edited by Luther Norris in the 1970s. His suggestion was to name the journal The Pontine Dossier Millenium edition and publish all-new Solar Pons essays from today's Pontine scholars. Thus, the concept for this journal was born.

This Dossier is the first of what we hope to be an annual publication, possibly even a twice annual depending on the interest from both the audience and the authors. Sherlock Holmes publications have always had a niche audience. Solar Pons's audience has been a niche of that niche. But as we know from our reissues of the original Derleth Pons books as well as our new collections of Solar Pons stories from David Marcum and others, that micro-audience is made up of rabid fans hungry for any and all things Pons.

We hope to quench the thirst of you admiring fans by continuing the Pontine Dossier far into the future.

May you always find a welcome home in Praed Street.

Sincerely,

Derrick Belanger, PSI ("Albert, the Dove")

Brian Belanger, PSI ("Sir Ronald Duveen")

P.S. – A special thank you goes out to all the authors in this first edition, George Vanderburgh for this brilliant idea, and especially to Danielle Hackett and Damon Derleth for allowing us to once again walk in the shadow of the Sherlock Holmes of Praed Street.

The World of August Derleth: Capturing the Spirit of Wisconsin Through Literature

By Chris Chan

INTRODUCTION: Who was August Derleth and why is his work relevant?

August Derleth (1909-1971) is one of the major figures in Wisconsin literature, and despite his relatively obscure status on the national stage; he has left an impression on various aspects of American fiction. He produced hundreds of books in nearly every style and genre imaginable, with the exception of drama. Indeed, he produced so much work that much of it is still being discovered in his voluminous archives and finally published long after his death. Despite the strikingly dissimilar natures of his books, one constant struggle permeates virtually every page he ever wrote: an attempt to capture the soul of Wisconsin and to share his fondness and enthusiasm with his readers.

Throughout Derleth's work, there is a powerful sense of love and appreciation for his home state. The Wisconsin terrain, the state's natural wonders, the eclectic population, local customs, and noteworthy events of Wisconsin's past and present were all close to Derleth's heart, and all of these elements served as major themes in Derleth's fiction. Even the Derleth works that are set in overseas countries or even alternative universes cover themes connected to Wisconsin. Like any individual viewpoint, Derleth's vision of Wisconsin is not all-encompassing, nor does Derleth present a picture of his home state that will satisfy everyone in terms of its accuracy and perception.

While Wisconsin was unquestionably a major formative influence on Derleth, it would be wrong to suggest that the state was the only influence on Derleth's mentality. Derleth's intellectual and religious backgrounds had similarly important impacts on his worldview and his writing. From his early youth onwards, Derleth embarked on a self-imposed educational reading program, and Derleth's Catholic faith also had a profound effect on him. He once declared that, "The principal influences of my formative years were Thoreau, Emerson, H.P. Lovecraft and H.L. Mencken, in that order; such Catholic influences as I am aware of are but two in number– Augustine and Jacques Maritain, though I ought not to discount my admiration for Hilaire Belloc, G.K. Chesterton, François Mauriac, and Msgr. Ronald Knox, among outstanding Catholic authors."[1]

This essay is an overview that places Derleth's vast quantity of writings into historical perspective. Derleth's literary output draws heavily upon Wisconsin's past and present. Social, political, and cultural connections to Wisconsin are inextricably woven into his work. Remarkably, historians and literary scholars have long overlooked Derleth's multifaceted career, and this essay will hopefully reveal

---

[1] August Derleth, "An Autobiography," <http://www.derleth.org/autobiog.htm> (3 December 2008).

a neglected facet of Wisconsin's intellectual and cultural history.

Derleth's career

Aspiring writers can regard Derleth's career simultaneously as a success story to be emulated and as a cautionary tale outlining potentially livelihood-endangering pitfalls. August Derleth produced so many volumes that he is frequently proclaimed to be Wisconsin's most prolific writer.[2] During his life, Derleth enjoyed a loyal fan base, consistent critical praise, and was widely respected for managing his career on his own terms. This high regard has continued over the decades following his death. At the same time, Derleth has been accused of putting quantity over quality, squandering his time on frivolous projects and genres, and repeatedly making decisions that were tantamount to career suicide, thereby costing him wider acclaim and leaving the overwhelming majority of his books out of print today.

Derleth is a legend throughout Wisconsin, particularly in the central region of the state, where he lived for nearly all of his life. Outside of Wisconsin, however, Derleth is almost completely unknown, aside from amongst devotees of his supernatural and detective fiction. Derleth's genre work, most notably his science fiction and mysteries, have earned him cult followings around the world. The rest of his work, composed primarily of two series of books that are popularly referred to as the Sac Prairie and Wisconsin Sagas,

---

[2] James P. Roberts, Famous Wisconsin Authors (Oregon, Wisconsin: Badger Books Inc., 2002), 35.

remain obscure at the national and international levels. A handful of his horror and mystery stories were adapted for television for various anthology shows between the 1950's and early 1970's, and one suspense novel was adapted for the big screen, but aside from those, Hollywood has showed no interest whatsoever in adapting Derleth's work.[3]

Derleth never received a Pulitzer Prize or a National Book Award, or even a nomination from any of the major literary prize-awarding organizations, save for one unsuccessful nod from the Mystery Writers of America for *The Memoirs of Solar Pons* and for winning a $2,500 Guggenheim Prize after receiving a nomination from Sinclair Lewis.[4] Although the Guggenheim Prize money was supposed to be used in order to fund travel expenses and to engage in various literary activities. Derleth wound up using that money in order to bind and preserve his comic collection. Throughout his professional life, Derleth would both defend and subvert literary perceptions and prejudices regarding highbrow, middlebrow, and lowbrow tastes.

A question therefore arises as to whether or not Derleth is worthy of serious study. Is a locally popular author of several scores of books, known for his fondness of genres frequently held in disrepute by mainstream critics, who has fallen into relative obscurity for decades, deserving of scholarly examination? It should come as no surprise that this essay will answer

---

[3] "August Derleth," The Internet Movie Database, < http://www.imdb.com/name/ nm0220421/> (4 December 2008).
[4] John Howard, "The Huge Newness of the Scene, 1937-39," <http://www.waldeneast. fsnet.co.uk/adp5.htm> (3 December 2008).

this question with an unequivocal "yes," after all, the reverse answer would mean that this study would never have been considered, let alone written.

August Derleth's career is indeed important for multiple reasons. First of all, he is a vital resource for anyone wishing to learn more about the social and cultural history of Wisconsin. Derleth's career is significant for his attempts to explore the Wisconsin experience through the medium of literature. Wisconsin has produced a number of notable writers, but only a handful of Wisconsin-born writers have been able to launch a sustainable writing career while remaining in their home state.

Derleth's greatest achievements were all rooted in one abiding principle: his lasting love for his home state. By portraying his home state through various perspectives through a variety of storylines, he sought to make others, both native Wisconsinites and outsiders, fall in love with his home.

Derleth and his vision of Wisconsin.

In his introduction to his book *Writing Fiction*, Derleth mused about the nature of the connection between the author and his creative work, writing that:

> "From the point of view of the writer, be he amateur or professional, all fiction falls into two general groups. These may be specified as realistic fiction on the one hand, and fiction which grows out of reality, on the other. These are broad classifications, and need little explanation, for it is obvious

that realistic fiction is that which not only could be true in every aspect, but in many cases is, the writer having drawn upon his experience or that of others in creating it; fiction which grows out of reality may range from the simple romantic all the way to the fantastic. So long as recognizable symbols are used by the writer. Reduced to its basic essential, fiction is life, interpreted realistically or imaginatively."[5]

This declaration is in some ways Derleth's artistic manifesto. He knew what he wanted to write about– the culture that built him and his neighbors.

Due to the immense size and diversity of Derleth's works, Derleth was frequently nicknamed "The Wisconsin Balzac."[6] Indeed, the writer Zealia Bishop used this moniker as the title of an essay she wrote on Derleth's career. Honoré de Balzac, the nineteenth-century French author is best known for his mammoth series of novels and short stories, commonly referred to as *The Human Comedy*. Over the course of nearly a hundred tales, Balzac presented an epic depiction of the various segments of French society set during the first half of the nineteenth century. Balzac, like Derleth, focused on the human factor, exploring individuals' psyches and responses to various events, with a special focus on themes like religion, culture, and

---

[5] August Derleth, <u>Writing Fiction</u> (Boston: The Writer, Inc. Publishers, 1946), v.

[6] Zealia Bishop, <u>The Curse of Yig and Others</u> (Sauk City, Wisconsin: Arkham House, 1953). 1-175.

morality. Derleth's Sac Prairie and Wisconsin Sagas, like Balzac's *Human Comedy*, were such gargantuan projects that neither author could finish his magnum opus: both authors left many works unfinished. Derleth's frequent themes of the culture, population, and topography of Wisconsin rank him as both a panoramic regionalist and a historical novelist.

Derleth's work covers the history of Wisconsin in numerous ways. Derleth's books can be categorized into several groups. Three main branches of Derleth's oeuvre are relevant to his artistic presentation of the history of Wisconsin. The first of these is his Sac Prairie Saga, a collection of novels, short stories, memoirs, history, and poetry regarding his home county. The Sac Prairie Saga covers both the past and present in Wisconsin history, covering the social, intellectual, and political forces that shape society. The second is the Wisconsin saga, a similar collection of books revolving around the whole of the state of Wisconsin, often focusing on real-life influential figures and how their careers affected the state. Finally, the third category of Derleth's fiction is largely underappreciated, since it centers on the works that are not generally categorized as "serious." Despite the fact that genre fiction is stereotypically held in lower regard than "straight" fiction, Derleth peppered his fantasy and mystery fiction with references to major issues facing Wisconsin, as well as editorializing on pressing problems for the state.

Derleth had a strong connection to Wisconsin's land, believing that the environment had a distinct and palpable effect on the people who lived there. Throughout his career, Derleth insisted that he had a moral duty to present the region in a way that was beautiful, yet was still honest and accurate. When discussing the artistic hazards of regional writing, Derleth editorialized,

> "It is true that, fundamentally, people are very much the same, but there are environmental differences which emerge tellingly in various regions, and there are economic problems, like those of sharecropping, industrialization, the Dust Bowl tragedy, etc., which are specifically regional, and people are profoundly affected by them. The writer of regional prose must know what has gone into the history of his region, what has influenced his people, what is responsible for their thought-patterns; he must know, in short, what specific problems determine what they say and do, and fix the patterns of their lives... A good regional novel is not written solely out of dialect differences, for instance; nor is it written out of quaint customs."[7]

This provides a glimpse at what Derleth was trying to accomplish by writing about his hometown. Derleth wanted to immortalize his home and show what made it special and interesting. In order to capture the soul of his beloved town and state, he needed to immerse himself in their history.

---

[7] Derleth, Writing Fiction, 14.

Evaluating and ranking Derleth's career.

In order to understand whether or not August Derleth's work is truly influential and worthy of serious study, it is necessary to explore the definition of a "serious" author, and consider the impact and achievements of his work.

One useful definition of a "serious" writer is an author whose work calls out for serious and thoughtful consideration, both for matters of artistic merit and for the messages expressed in the work. "Serious," then, is not used in this context as an antithesis of "funny" or "entertaining."

Talented authors become "great" writers through two sources: the first being through the quality of their work, the second being the critical and fan base that promotes and defends their writing. Derleth's unconventional career may have hampered his wider reputation. There are numerous authors who are classified as "minor" writers of note. This vaguely appreciative yet simultaneously patronizing term is often attributed to writers who have substantial fan bases yet for various reasons have not enjoyed the full adulation of the critical pantheon. At this moment, Derleth is considered a major figure in Wisconsin's literary life, but on the national scene he is a very minor figure indeed, although he is frequently cited as a significant Midwestern regionalist.

Many notable American writers have been regionalists. Willa Cather's reputation rests on her depiction of the American West, William Faulkner and Eudora Welty set most of their work in Mississippi,

Flannery O'Connor's work draws heavily on Southern life, and much of Saul Bellow's fiction is set in urban Chicago. It is not surprising that Wisconsin has inspired regionalist work by Derleth and other scribes, but what is thought provoking is the question as to why hardly any of these Wisconsin authors has gained a particularly prominent role on the national and international literary stage. Could the answer for this failure lie in talent issues, simple luck, or just provincialist prejudice?

At times, Derleth felt that the answer lay in the last possibility, and that his being a committed Wisconsinite might have stunted the growth of his career. Early in his career, Derleth was on the fast track to literary prominence by virtue of being taken under the wing of Maxwell Perkins, a respected New York editor who had worked with legendary writers such as Ernest Hemingway and F. Scott Fitzgerald. Perkins and Derleth had sharply opposing ideas regarding the future of the young writer's career, and eventually Derleth decided that he could not conform to Perkins' expectations of how a leading American author ought to direct his career. Apparently, Derleth's fascination with genre and his unwillingness to abandon rural Sac Prairie for the fashionable literary circles of New York doomed the business relationship, and from then on, Derleth would direct his own career.[8] He would never gain the level of celebrity that he might have had he allowed himself to be molded into Perkins's image, but Derleth was always and immutably his own man.

Understanding the critical milieu in which Derleth struggled is vital to determining whether or not

---

[8] Roberts, 37.

Derleth's stress on all things Wisconsin-related affected the trajectory of his career. That is why it is necessary to cover the contemporary critical response to Derleth's work, through reviews and other criticisms, and then synthesize these viewpoints in order to see how well they approximate the real man.

Derleth and his challenge to literary standards.

Although Derleth never launched a full-out attack on contemporary literary mores, much of his work involved some overt criticism of mainstream standards. Derleth's career was in many ways based on a battle with literary standards. Although he sometimes accepted the dominant critical paradigm that accepted only "serious" fiction as "high" culture worthy of respect, preservation, and admiration; and derided "entertainment" fiction, such as mysteries, fantasies, and largely humorous pieces, as at best frivolous diversions and at worst mere trash. In this critical estimation, genre fiction and second-class or lower writing, was identifiable and innately inferior to "serious" fiction. This perspective has been in critical vogue ever since the ascendance of literary modernism. The qualifying of who is worthy to become an arbiter of culture is a hotly contentious one, and Derleth would pose numerous challenges to prevailing standards throughout his career. At the front of his assault on standard literary mores was his defense and celebration of genre fiction.

Derleth did not call for the apotheosis of all genre fiction, but he did insist that the best-written fantasy and crime work should receive more critical respect. In an essay on the state of contemporary science fiction, he wrote, "[S]ome contemporary science-fiction is making a serious claim to consideration as literature in the same classification as the more meritorious stories of crime and general adventure. But this is as yet only a very small percentage of the science-fiction written or being written...its claim to literary distinction must rest on a small minority of the books and stories in the genre."[9] When Derleth did find work he deemed worthy of celebrating, he threw himself heart and soul into promoting and defending it.

In many ways, Derleth was one of the earliest– and most successful– "fanboys." In contemporary terminology, a fanboy is a person with a devotion to some sort of entertainment, such as an author's work, a television show, or a movie franchise. The word often has a slightly derisive implication, implying that the person in question could find more worthwhile ways in which to spend his time. The subject of the fanboy's obsession is usually a form of genre, such as fantasy, science fiction, or mystery. Fanboys are known for devoting most of their spare time enjoying, studying, and popularizing their fixation, often with others with similar interests.

Today, many fanboys spend their free time writing fanfiction, where they expand upon the mythos of their favorite stories and characters. Fanfiction is usually illegal, except in cases of parody and public domain fictional universes. Therefore, most fanfiction is published anonymously on the Internet, and fanfiction writers almost invariably never make a penny for their

---

[9] August Derleth, "Contemporary Science Fiction," The English Journal 41 no. 1, (January, 1952): 7.

time and effort. Derleth was an extreme rarity: he was both able to publish his fanfiction in book form and use the profits to sustain his personal finances while he wrote literature with less commercial appeal. There were two prominent examples of Derleth building his career upon fanfiction. In the first, Derleth added to the fantastical world created by H.P. Lovecraft, who was not only one of his favorite authors, but was also his friend and correspondent. The most popular branch of Lovecraft's oeuvre consists of the stories about the Great Old Ones, a collection of mostly malevolent godlike monsters with assorted powers, and their frequently devastating effects on the lives of New Englanders. In Lovecraft's original tales, the Great Old Ones provoke chaos and destruction, and the moral overtones of the series reflect Lovecraft's atheistic worldview. When Derleth made his additions to the Cthulhu Mythos (a term coined by Derleth, named after the most popular of the Great Old Ones), he changed the morals of the tales to reflect his own Catholic faith, and instead of nihilism, Derleth's tales had a decidedly moral overtone, where the forces of goodness clashed with the forces of evil.

The second important example of Derleth's successful fanfiction was his Solar Pons stories. Derleth was an enthusiastic fan of the mysteries of Sir Arthur Conan Doyle. When Doyle decided to retire from writing the Sherlock Holmes series, Derleth wrote to Doyle and asked Doyle if he could take over the series for him.[10] When this literary correspondence failed to blossom into a friendship as it did with Lovecraft, Derleth decided to channel his ideas for new Holmes

---

[10] Roberts, 36.

mysteries into pastiches with his own detective, Solar Pons, which is an approximation of what the name "Sherlock Holmes" sounds like when spoken with a very heavy lisp. As a character, Solar Pons is not a parody of Holmes so much as he is an extreme fan of the great detective who has modeled himself after his hero, and who possesses similarly amazing powers of observation and deduction. Pons's friends and associates mirror Holmes's circle of allies, and indeed, Pons and Holmes coexist in the same fictional universe, with the two collaborating on certain cases that are referred to but never recounted. Throughout the Pons stories, Derleth introduces some of his other favorite fictional characters in cameo appearances, and Pons frequently pontificates on certain social issues that reflect topics that were being debated in Wisconsin at the time, such as criminal justice reform. Derleth continued to experiment with the genre, for unlike the Holmes mysteries, on occasion the supernatural is an integral part of the solution to the mysteries.

Both Derleth's Pons mysteries and his continuations of Lovecraft's fictional mythology have earned him cult followings, but the hidden ideological themes inside them have rarely been analyzed, nor have their ties to Wisconsin's history and society been given serious attention.

CONCLUSION: Why Derleth matters.

August Derleth is an important subject of consideration for any study of the cultural history of Wisconsin. No other Wisconsin writer has ever been as prolific as he was in presenting the state through the written word, and few other states in America have a resident author who has mirrored his career. Furthermore, Derleth's career is important for those studying twentieth-century American intellectual and cultural history, due to his opinions on cultural trends, as well as his experimentations with the form.

Derleth's life, work, and legacy need to be considered from multiple aspects in order for it to be thoroughly evaluated. Earlier studies of Derleth's work have tended to either focus solely on his "serious" fiction, mentioning his other writings only in passing, or to be primarily fan-driven and unscholarly musings on his genre work, without any reference to his Wisconsin-based books.

Even when Derleth attempted to recreate the streets of London or embellish fantasy words controlled by malevolent supernatural forces, he brought the concerns facing Wisconsin and commentary on pressing issues into play. From the Sac Prairie-set Judge Peck mysteries, to the editorial monologues delivered by Solar Pons, to the moral lessons woven into his take on the Cthulhu Mythos, Derleth permeated his work with Wisconsin-related concerns, as well as his personal opinions and worldviews. Derleth's mysteries and fantasy fiction are almost invariably overlooked in the handful of scholarly studies of his work, partially due to the widespread prejudice against genre fiction.

Derleth once commented,

> "[T]he writer who is impelled toward imaginative fiction as his forte, will be advised to keep at least one foot solidly on familiar ground. Anything

out of the ordinary is so much more effective in a familiar setting. Explaining his own credo, H.P. Lovecraft... wrote in 1931: "To make a fictional marvel wear the momentary aspect of exciting fact, we must give it the most elaborate possible approach– building it up insidiously and gradually out of apparently realistic material, realistically handled... In every detail *except* the chosen marvel, the story should be accurately true to nature... Spectral fiction should be realistic as well as atmospheric– confining its departure from nature to the one supernatural channel chosen, and remembering that scene, mood, and phenomena are more important in conveying what is to be conveyed than are characters and plot."[11]

When he wrote this, Derleth explained his own rationalizations behind inserting so many of his Wisconsin-related themes into his genre fiction. In his attempt to be "true to nature" and "realistic," Derleth needed to incorporate his own familiar world into the fantastical fictional universes he created, sometimes by mirroring themes, controversies, or individuals.

For Derleth, Wisconsin was a world onto itself, a rich and unique microcosm that was emblematic of the nation's social foundations. Sac Prairie was special to

---

[11] Derleth, Writing Fiction, 97.

him, but it was supposedly representative of the entire American small-town experience. In his book <u>Village Year: A Sac Prairie Journal,</u> Derleth wrote, "Life in Sac Prairie cannot differ much from life in any other village, apart from superficial regional differences."[12] Nearly all of his writings explore the some aspect of what it meant to be a Wisconsinite, ranging from one's interactions with one's neighbors to the lasting effects of the political system on the average citizen.

To conclude this introduction to Derleth's work, it should be reiterated that Derleth was unquestionably a Wisconsinite. While it might be too much of a stretch to contend that his place of residence was the primary molding influence upon his character– after all, religion and reading material shaped his intellectual bent to an incalculable extent– it is reasonable to contend that Derleth made a definite choice to use all sorts of Wisconsin-related aspects to form the backbone of his literary output. It is impossible to tell if Derleth would have shaped his career around regionalism had he been born and raised in New England or the Pacific coast or the Deep South. Perhaps Derleth might have written sagas set in any of the aforementioned places had he lived in one of them, or perhaps there was simply something about Wisconsin that appealed to his mental make-up. Even if it is impossible to determine the specific reasons why Sac Prairie was dear to Derleth, the fact remains that Sac Prairie struck Derleth at a deep-seated emotional level. In his introduction to *Walden*

---

[12] August Derleth, <u>Village Year: A Sac Prairie Journal</u> (New York: Coward-McCann, Inc., 1941), xii.

West, Derleth describes the overwhelming visceral effect that his hometown had on him:

> "A time came three decades ago, when I found I must choose between going out into the wider world or traveling widely in the microcosms of Sac Prairie. I had been away from Sac Prairie scarcely half a year, immured in a city at editorial work, and I could ill bear separation from the village, the river, the hills, and the lowlands among which I had put down roots and with which I had come to terms of a sort...
>
> When the opportunity came, I went back to Sac Prairie without regret... So I set about to write so that I might afford the leisure in which to improve my acquaintance with the setting and the inhabitants– hills, trees, ponds, people, birds, animals, sun, moon, stars– of the region I had chosen to inhabit, not as a retreat, but as a base of operations into a life more full in the knowledge of what went on in the woods as well as in the houses along the streets if Sac Prairie and in the human heart."[13]

These lines from *Walden West* summarize the aspects that so enamored Sac Prairie to Derleth. As

---

[13] August Derleth, Walden West (Madison: The University of Wisconsin Press, 1961), xv.

Derleth states in the above passage, Sac Prairie was Derleth's personal corner of the world, and it gave him the inspiration for launching his literary career. Any study of August Derleth's career needs to center on more than just his own life, but his beloved Sac Prairie, Wisconsin, and his conceptions of the nature of literature as well.

*****

Works Cited

"August Derleth." The Internet Movie Database. < http://www.imdb.com/name/ nm0220421/> (4 December 2008).

Bishop, Zealia. The Curse of Yig and Others. Sauk City, Wisconsin: Arkham House, 1953.

Derleth, August. "An Autobiography." <http://www.derleth.org/autobiog.htm> (3 December 2008).

—————— "Contemporary Science Fiction." The English Journal 41 no. 1. (January, 1952): 1-8.

—————— Village Year: A Sac Prairie Journal. New York: Coward-McCann, Inc., 1941.

—————— Walden West. Madison: The University of Wisconsin Press, 1961.

—————— Writing Fiction. Boston: The Writer, Inc. Publishers, 1946.

Howard, John. "The Huge Newness of the Scene, 1937-39." <http://www.waldeneast.fsnet.co.uk/adp5.htm> (3 December 2008).

Roberts, James P. Famous Wisconsin Authors. Oregon, Wisconsin: Badger Books Inc., 2002.

Wilson, Alison M. August Derleth: A Bibliography. Metuchen, New Jersey: The Scarecrow Press, Inc., 1983.

*****

Biographical note about the author:

Chris Chan is a writer and educator. He is a researcher and "International Goodwill Ambassador" for Agatha Christie Ltd., and writes for *Gilbert!* and *The Strand.* He is also the author of the Funderburke mystery series.

But Was She a Vampire?

By Derrick Belanger, PSI

While all of Dr. Parker's retellings of the adventures of his dear friend Solar Pons show the seemingly extra-normal mental abilities of the Praed Street detective, these feats are grounded in the real world. There is nothing paranormal about them. Whether he deduces a document is fabricated from a crooked typed letter "q" or figures out a woman is guilty of murder from the lipstick found in her purse, it is Pons's ratiocination that he uses to draw his conclusions. As magical as Mr. Pons seems, his talents come not from the spiritual realm but from the art of detection.

There are, however, several adventures which hint at powers beyond the abilities of Mr. Pons, powers which go beyond the realms of accepted science. One such case is "The Adventure of the Nosferatu" (collected in *The Apocrypha of Solar Pons*), which concludes that the villain of the story is a vampire. The story revolves around the case of Dr. Poula Couty, a woman, Pons claims, who is "*Nosferatu*...somewhat more than four hundred years of age." But is Pons telling the truth? Is there perhaps a different reason for Pons making this claim and for Dr. Parker publishing the story, a story with no apparent mystery and no clear conclusion?

To puzzle out the truth behind this story, one must first look at the facts of the narrative and the time period in which it was published. The story first appeared in the 1950's at the height of the Cold War and begins with Pons and Parker debating the merits of mythical beasts. Pons argues that all myths have a basis in reality. Parker counters that beasts such as Centaurs do not. Pons scoffs at this and lectures Parker that the Centaurs were a Greek clan of horsemen. As the clan died out, their artwork depicting the image of the Centaur we know survived, and the legend of the Centaur slowly developed over time.

The narrative then shifts as a client arrives in Praed Street. Pons and Parker are visited by an American named David Bentley, who tells them that he is in London to hunt a vampire. The vampire is Dr. Poula Coty, an esteemed, beautiful woman with connections to the Hague. Bentley claims that Coty is a bloodthirsty monster who tricked and murdered his friend James Grunland, a man who also sought to hunt down the creature. Pons appears to take Bentley seriously and agrees to accept the case on the condition that Bentley not shoot Dr. Coty (he is armed with a gun containing silver bullets). Bentley agrees – at least he won't shoot the doctor until after he visits with Pons again.

After Bentley leaves, Pons tells Parker that there could be some truth to Bentley's story. "Dr. Coty is prominent," Pons explains, "but prominence is no guarantee that she is not also a murderess." Once again, we have Pons declaring that there is some truth behind a myth. He also tells Parker that he thinks Bentley is unhinged. Dr. Coty surely is not a vampire.

Several days later Bentley returns and explains to Pons and Parker that he was wrong about Dr. Coty. Pons assumes Bentley means that he has come to his senses and realizes the woman isn't a vampire, but then Bentley explains Dr. Coty is most certainly a vampire, just not a murderer. Bentley goes on to retell of his visit to Dr. Coty, how she was incredibly beautiful and how she admitted that she is a vampire but that the legends of evil vampires are just that, legends. She told Bentley that his friend Grunland had helped her to stay alive, willingly donating his blood to the vampire.

After hearing this story, Pons travels to the Hague for a few days. He returns to discover that Bentley, like his friend, has willingly given himself up to Dr. Coty. It is at this point when Pons reveals that Dr. Coty really is a Nosferatu and that she is on a sinister mission, a "mission that involves bringing her fellows into a prominence in the affairs of the world." Pons tells Parker that they must work together to stop her. The detective gets Parker to promise not to publish whatever transpires in the remainder of the case, that it must remain secret. Thus, unsatisfactorily, comes the end of an adventure which really has just begun.

Why Publish This Case?

With Pons asking Parker not to publish the majority of the Nosferatu adventure, it begs the question as to why Parker published the exploit at all. The narrative is no more than a fragment which ends with the revelation that vampires walk the earth, a revelation which Pons seems not to want Parker to share. Why would the detective approve of Parker revealing that vampires exist but not approve of him saying how he and Pons defeated them? From a literary and logical perspective, the story makes no sense. But what if that's the point? What if the sense was that the story makes no sense? What if there was there an underlying message intended for a specific audience, an audience beyond Parker's typical readership?

An answer can be found in several of the adventures of Solar Pons. We know that Pons worked closely with his brother Bancroft who, like his predecessor Mycroft Holmes, at times was *the* British government. Bancroft worked against the Germans during both World Wars and then against the Russians during the Cold War. We know he was concerned with spies and espionage. We also know that a number of Pons stories connect to forgeries (Unique Dickensians) and cyphers (Terror Over London), tactics with major implications throughout the Cold War.

What does this have to do with a narrative about a vampire? The answer is that Solar Pons and Dr. Parker were using the story to convey a message. The argument at the beginning of the story between Pons and Parker clearly explains that there is a kernel of truth behind myths. This is a message to the story's intended audience, a cypher within the British government or perhaps a spy working for Her Majesty's Secret Service, that there is upcoming information in the adventure which will be of utmost importance to the commonwealth. The message, though, is hinted at and not clearly explained. Pons needed to make sure that the British agent would understand the message but a foreign agent would only see an odd story about a detective fighting an undead monster.

The character of Bentley most likely represents an American agent who worked with Pons. His friend Grunland was another American agent who he believed had been killed by the enemy, the enemy represented by Dr. Coty who was in actuality a Russian mole who had infiltrated the British government. Pons's explanation to Parker that there was some truth to Bentley's story, that even though Coty has risen to prominence, it doesn't mean that she is not a murderer, i.e. because she is respected, doesn't mean she isn't a Russian agent.

When Bentley explains that Grunland willingly died for Dr. Coty, he is revealing that either Grunland has always been a Russian mole or that he has been flipped and is now working for the Russians. Eventually, Bentley is also turned to Coty's side. This is a message that there are multiple Russian agents working for the British government. Most likely, these characters are described in ways which identify their real-life counterparts.

Pons's explanation at the end of the adventure that he has gone to the Hague and discovers that Dr. Coty is really a vampire is a code to identify the head of the Russian spies who have infiltrated the government. Whoever Dr. Coty truly is, whether one man or woman or code name for a team, she has infiltrated the highest levels of the British government and must be stopped before she reveals all of their secrets to the enemy. Pons rallies Parker to his side and says that they must defeat this Nosferatu and her kind. In the end, Pons is warning his compatriots that they need to defeat Dr. Coty before it is too late.

Why stop on a cliffhanger ending? Because Pons is showing that until Coty and her agents are stopped, Britain isn't safe. The fact that Britain did not fall in the 1950s is evidence that Pons was successful in capturing the enemy agents and saving the British government. If Pons was not on the case, perhaps the ending of the Cold War would have been much different.

*****

Biographical note about the author:

Derrick Belanger, PSI is an author and educator most noted for his books and lectures on Sherlock Holmes and Sir Arthur Conan Doyle, as well as his writing for the blogs *I Hear of Sherlock Everywhere* and *Belanger Books Sherlock Holmes and Other Readings Blog*. Both volumes of his two-volume anthology, *A Study in Terror: Sir Arthur Conan Doyle's Revolutionary Stories of Fear and the Supernatural* were #1 best sellers on the Amazon.com U.K. Sherlock Holmes book list, and his *MacDougall Twins with Sherlock Holmes* chapter book, *Attack of the Violet Vampire!* was also a #1 bestselling new release in the U.K. Through his press, Belanger Books, he has released a number of Sherlock Holmes anthologies as well as new editions of August Derleth's original Solar Pons series. In 2019, Mr. Belanger received his investiture in the PSI as "Albert, the Dove". Mr. Belanger's academic work has been published in *The Colorado Reading Journal* and *Gifted Child Today*. Find him at www.belangerbooks.com.

How Deep Did the Amworthy Hoax Go?

By James C. O'Leary, PSI

Circa 1930, Solar Pons declared that the books listed in the four page brochure for the Amworthy Auction "have a precarious existence only in the writings of certain minor authors of American origin, all apparently followers, in a remote sense, of the work of Edgar Allan Poe. The catalogue is, in short, a hoax." We shall see that Pons's own statement about the Amworthy Catalog was spurious. It certainly could not have been made at the time Dr. Lyndon Parker tells us it was made. Nor, if Pons's assertion were true, could it have been used for the purpose of fooling six of "the best-known collectors of occult lore in the British Isles." Why, then was Pons recorded as saying this? How, also, do we square this with the thumbnail biography of Pons that we have from Parker's literary agent, August Derleth, which all Pontine scholars accept as true?

Hoax?

Parker tells us that 6SIL occurred "in October early in the fourth decade of this century" while Pons says that the Fortsas Hoax took place some "ninety years ago...in August, 1840." So, then it seems certain that 6SIL happened in 1930, or 1931 at the latest. With those dates in mind, an in depth look at the books from the catalog mentioned in the adventure is in order. "In the case of the title which heads the list," according to Baron de Baseuil, "every reputed fact supposedly 'known' about this rare volume has been skillfully added to the customary one always finds in descriptions of books up for sale to make the paragraph, thus lending it still more superficial reality."

Al Hazred, Abdul: *Necronomicon*. **[Al Hazred is first mentioned in "The Nameless City" by Howard Philips Lovecraft (HLP) published November 1921** *The Wolverine*. **"The Hound" HPL February 1924** *Weird Tales* **first mentions his authorship.]** Tr. From the Arabic in to Latin by Olaus Wormius. With several woodcut tables of signs and mystic symbols. Madrid, 1647. **["The Festival" HPL January 1925** *Weird Tales* **mentions Olaus Wormius.]** Small folio, full calf with ornamental overall stamping in blind, including date, 1715. Binding somewhat stained and rubbed. In find condition, and only one of six known copies if the first Latin edition. Only copies known to be in existence are in the Bibliotheque Nationale of Paris, the Widener Library at Harvard, and Miskatonic University Library at Arkham, Massachusetts, U.S.A. **[Those libraries as well as the British Museum and the University of Buenos Ayres are mentioned in HPL's "The Dunwich Horror" April 1929** *Weird Tales*. **If the British Museum had been mentioned in the catalog then it is possible that the Baron either could have known whether the** *Necronomicon* **existed before hand or could have check the Museum on if it existed or not.]** Only privately owned copy known to have been in existence disappeared from the library of the Massachusetts artist, R. U. Pickman. **["Pickman's**

Model" HPL October 1927 *Weird Tales*. "Pickman's Model" does not mention *The Necronomicon*; Pickman's ownership is mentioned in HPL's "History of the *Necronomicon*" written 1927, posthumously published in 1938. It also contains all the facts mentioned above.]** Only two copies in Arabic known to have existed. According to Von Junzt in *Unausprechlichen Kulten* (see number 17, page four this catalog) *"es steht ausser Zweifel, dass dieses Buch ist die Grundlage der Okkulteliteratur."* **[*Unausprechlichen Kulten* Robert E. Howard (REH), "Children of the Night" April-May 1931 Weird Tales. HLP mentions *Unausprechlichen Kulten* and *Book of Eibon* in "The Dreams in the Witch House" July 1933 *Weird Tales*.]**

The other books mentioned: d'Erlette, Paul Henri, Comte de*: Cultes des Goules*, Rouen, 1737 **["The Suicide in the Study" Robert Bloch (RB), June 1935 *Weird Tales*. HPL mentions *Cultes* in "The Shadow Out of Time" June 1936 *Astounding Stories*]**; Prinn, Ludvig: *De Vermis Mysteriis*, Prague, 1807 **["*The Shambler from the Stars*" RB, September 1935 *Weird Tales*]**; *Liber Ivonis* (Author unknown), Rome, 1662. **[First mentioned, as the *Book of Eibon*, in "The Return of the Sorcerer" Clark Ashton Smith (CAS), September 1931 *Strange Tales of Mystery and Terror*. "The Haunter of the Dark" HPL December 1936 *Weird Tales* first mention of the Latinized title.]**

Lovecraft (1890-1937) maintained a voluminous correspondence with his fellow horror writers Howard, Bloch, Smith, and Parker's own literary agent Derleth. HPL encouraged his friends to utilize his growing, yet as of the early 1930s, unnamed mythos. They shared manuscripts before publication among themselves, and at times, Lovecraft would incorporate bits of his friend's mythologies into his work before they had published them. HPL also had a revision business on the side, revising other writer's works sometimes to the point that the original author's contribution was miniscule.

Lin Carter, in *Lovecraft: A Look Behind the "Cthulhu Mythos,"* writes, "Probably the first of [HPL's] friends to [contribute to the Mythos] was Clark Ashton Smith. In the September 1931 issue of *Strange Tales*, Smith published a very successful horror story called The Return of the Sorcerer....And there, smack in the middle of a story by Smith, baffled readers encountered a long passage of ominous and enigmatic Alhazredic prose, which must have roused questions in their minds, such as: If two different writers quote from the same book, is it possible that the *Necronomicon* is a real book?" "The Nameless Offspring" of June 1932's *Strange Tales* also contained a long passage from the *Necronomicon*. The HPL revision "Out of the Eons" by Hazel Heald ("I imagine it is at least 60 percent Lovecraft," says Carter.), April 1935 *Weird Tales,* mentions the *Necronomicon*, Cthulhu, Tsathoggua, *Unaussprechlichen Kulten*, the *Book of Eibon*, the Tcho-Tchos and Gnoph-keh, some tropes which only in retrospect will be recognized as parts of the Mythos.

It seems that only by the mid-1930s would a pulp horror fan perceive the existence of certain minor American authors writing in a shared horror universe. Forgoing the fact that some of the Amworthy catalog titles did not yet exist in print in 1930 or 1931, would six of England's best-known occult collectors be fooled by titles that only appeared within the last ten years in somewhat obscure horror pulps? And where does that leave Pons' 1931 monograph *An Examination of the Cthulhu Cult and Others*? Is it a work of literary criticism; the first examination of Lovecraft and friends' still-growing body of work?

It is impossible that perhaps-future forger Alastair White, in 1930 or '31, be aware of the books of the Cthulhu mythos listed in his catalog—even if he were a member of Lovecraft's correspondence circle. It is impossible that *all* six of England's greatest occult collectors be duped by such fictitious titles; certainly, Baron de Baseuil seems intelligent. It is impossible that Pons could write a treatise on Lovecraftian literature focusing on Cthulhu to be published in 1931.

There is only the improbable. That there was a circle "of certain minor authors of American origin, all apparently followers, in a remote sense, of the work of Edgar Allan Poe," who wrote fiction with mentions of the *Necronomicon, Unaussprechlichen Kulten, Cultes des Goules, De Vermis Mysteriis* and *Liber Ivonis*; and that the *Necronomicon, Unaussprechlichen Kulten, Cultes des Goules, De Vermis Mysteriis* and *Liber Ivonis* did, and does, exist. Those five grimoires being real would account for the collectors (or their representatives) traveling to Edinburgh to purchase them. Lovecraft included real titles linked to the occult and supernatural, such as *Ars Magna et Ultima, Book of Dzyan, Daemonolatreia,* various titles by Cotton Mather, in with his fictional titles. It can be supposed that Lovecraft shared the little-known but very real five titles later used by Alistair White with his circle who then fictionalized them in their own stories.

Then, it is also probable that Pons's title is a work relating to cultists who worshiped Cthulhu and their intersection with crime. Pons's personal knowledge of the cult came from his time in the Pacific South Seas at the beginning of the twentieth century which culminated with his monograph *An Inquiry into the Nan-Matal Ruins of Ponape* (1905).

A South Seas Sojourn

In HPL's "The Call of Cthulhu" (*Weird Tales*, February 1928), an article in the *Sydney Bulletin* from April 18, 1925, recounts the adventures of a Norwegian named Gustaf Johansen, second mate onboard the *Emma*. It encountered a heavily-armed yacht, the *Alert*, which attacked without provocation. In the ensuing battle the *Emma* was lost and the surviving crew killed the *Alert* crew and commandeered their ship. On board the *Alert* is a strange idol of a being, "a monster of vaguely anthropoid outline, but with an octopus-like head whose face was a mass of feelers, a scaly, rubbery-looking body, prodigious claws on hind and fore feet, and long, narrow wings behind. This thing... was of a somewhat bloated corpulence, and squatted evilly on a rectangular block or pedestal covered with undecipherable characters. The tips of the wings touched the back edge of the block, the seat occupied the centre, whilst the long, curved claws of the doubled-up, crouching hind legs gripped the front edge and extended a quarter of the way down toward the bottom of the pedestal. The cephalopod head was bent forward, so that the ends of the facial feelers brushed the backs of huge fore paws which clasped the croucher's elevated knees." This, by the way, was identical to an idol found by Inspector John Raymond Legrasse, New Orleans Police Department when he rounded up some cultist in the Louisiana bayous in 1908. The cultists, responsible for some grizzly human sacrifices to this idol, had been chanting *"Ph'nglui mglw'nafh Cthulhu R'lyeh wgah'nagl fhtagn,"* the identical chant that "the late William Channing Webb, Professor of Anthropology in Princeton University" had recorded devil-worshiping Esquimaux in West Greenland chanting in 1860 and to a similar idol.

The *Emma*'s crew continued on their journey and the next day came upon an island that had recently been risen from the ocean floor by the March 1 earthquake, in the vicinity of 47°9′S 126°43′W. The crew went ashore to explore, and Johansen was the only survivor of the *Emma*'s crew of that trip. He refused to say what had happened, but he left a written record which was subsequently found. On a muddy landscape with "weedy Cyclopean masonry," Johansen and his crew encountered a giant, living version of the idol and only Johansen escaped with his life. Whether Johansen's handwritten account is truthful, Cyclopean ruins and the Pacific are associated with Cthulhu and some 5,100 nautical miles to the east of the uncharted, temporary island are the Cyclopean ruins of Ponape (now called Pohnpei).

Pons's early years before meeting his Boswell, Dr. Parker, are generally unknown, aside from Derleth's thumbnail biography. Put in chronological order: born c.

1880; graduate Oxford *summa cum laude* 1889; wrote *An Inquiry into the Nan-Matal Ruins of Ponape* 1905; established private inquiry practice 1907; British Intelligence World War I. Put in this order, the Ponape treatise seems out of place, unless archeology was one of his studies at Oxford. There is a tantalizing hint in *The Dragnet Solar Pons et al.* Introduction and Notes by Mark Wardecker. On page 8 is a photo of the typescript of the first page of "The Adventure of the Black Narcissus." In paragraph two, the original line reads, "Pons and I had been doing nothing all day—that is I was engaged in reading or writing, he in archeological investigations." "*I was*" was crossed out and penned above was "*we were*;" "*he in archeological investigations*" was crossed out and '*without other active occupation*" penned above, so that "Pons and I had been doing nothing all day—that is we were engaged in reading or writing without other active occupation" appeared in the February 1929 *The Dragnet Magazine*. For publication in the Mycroft & Moran "*In Re: Sherlock Holmes"—The Adventures of Solar Pons* (1945) the line became "Pons and I had been comparatively inactive that day; we read and wrote; I had little business, for my practice had not at that time taken on much significance."

There may be no significance to the change in wording other than authorial whim, but interest in archeology and criminal investigation seem to be of long standing. Both involve "digging" for evidence and assembling it to tell a coherent story. An inquiry into little-known Pacific ruins cannot be profitably conducted from an armchair so perforce Pons had to have traveled there. But the question arises, if Pons was serious enough about archeology to travel so short a time out of university, 8,250 miles, to the remote Pacific and write up his researches for publication in 1905, why then did he abandon that calling and become a private inquiry agent just two years later? Perhaps both types of investigation, archeological and investigatory, were involved in Pons's South Seas journey, through the offices of that man in His Majesty's Service, Bancroft Pons.

"Karolinen"

After German unification in 1871, the people started to see themselves as a nation, like Great Britain and France, and nations in those days had colonies. Germany started to build its Navy which would facilitate colonial acquisition and by the mid-1880s, German South West Africa and German New Guinea found their way onto the map followed by German East Africa and German West Africa in the '90s. German companies already had an influential presence in the Pacific, especially Deutsche Handels-und Plantagen-Gesellschaft der Südsee-Inseln zu Hamburg (DHPG) which carried a not-insignificant amount European trade to the area.

According to the National Library of Australia:

Intent on protecting German trading interests and taking advantage of British diplomatic weaknesses, the German Government annexed Kaiser Wilhelmsland (north eastern New Guinea) and the Bismarck Archipelago (New Britain and New Ireland) in 1884. The Marshall Islands and the northern Solomon Islands (Buka, Bougainville and other islands) were annexed in 1885.

From 1885 to 1899 German New Guinea was a protectorate ruled by the Neuguinea Kompagnie. The costs of administering the Marshall Islands, including Nauru, were borne by the DHPG. In 1898 the German Government agreed to take over the administration of New Guinea and a governor was appointed, based at Herbertshöhe (Kokopo) in New Britain. In 1906 the Marshall Islands became an administrative district of New Guinea. In 1910 the capital of the colony was moved to Rabaul.

> Samoa was always the centre of German commerce in the Pacific. In 1877, for instance, Germans had 87 per cent of the export trade from Samoa. In 1888 a native uprising under Mata'afa [Mata'afa Iosefo (1832 1912) a Paramount Chief of Samoa] and the ambush of a German naval party led the German consul in Apia to proclaim annexation. [Otto von] Bismarck was aware of British and American treaty rights and from 1889 onwards a tridominium administered Samoa. In 1899 civil war broke out and Mata'afa's forces gained control of the islands. Germany put pressure on Britain, which was facing problems in South Africa, and the Treaty of Berlin divided Samoa between Germany (the western islands) and the United States, with Britain gaining exclusive rights in Tonga.

Wilhelm Solf was appointed the first Governor of Samoa. At the same time, Spain, having lost the Philippines, ceded the Carolines, Palaus and Marianas to Germany in return for a payment. They were made administrative districts of German New Guinea.[14]

Ponape is in the Caroline Islands. Spanish rule had been particularly brutal, but Berlin, while having definite plans for the island, went out of their way not to provoke the Ponapeans, at least at first.

Britain, of course, was interested in the worldwide doings of Germany and Kaiser Wilhelm II, and in his brother Solar, Bancroft had the perfect man fort the perfect place. An archeological mystery in the Nan-Matal (now called Nan Madol) ruins built in the lagoon on the eastern side of the island and a German governor in Victor Berg (1861-1907) of a place with no more than 50 Europeans at any one time with a tendency towards impulsiveness versus a German-speaking Oxford grad who is interested in archeological and human puzzles.

Forty-year-old Berg took over from Ponape's first German governor, Albert Hahl, in 1901. He characterized Ponapeans as "incorrigible layabouts and ill-civilised Yankee apes."

Berg arrived with definite preconceptions about the job, and he

---

[14] "German Colonies in the Pacific," National Library of Australia, https://www.nla.gov.au/selected-library-collections/german-colonies-in-the-pacific

earned a severe censure from the Colonial Department within his first two months, after a rashly-worded dispatch announcing his determination to assert imperial authority 'forcefully' and to meet local resistance with 'relentless' reprisals. He learned his lesson very quickly, however, after his superiors warned that any unrest during his appointment would lead to an immediate recall. His administration thereafter was marked by a singular restraint and sobriety...[15]

Berg would have no doubt welcomed the company of the urbane Pons, talking of archeology and other topics and perhaps being indiscrete about German plans.

Denouement

Did Pons's investigation of the Nan Madol ruins uncover any Cthulhuiod connections? Without access to Pons' monograph one can only speculate, but it is doubtful. The structures do not date back eons but to 1180–1200 C.E. It is unlikely that Pons would have come to a radically different opinion. More likely is that Pons would have heard whispers about the cult from some beachcomber that washed up on the Ponape shore

---

[15] Hempenstall, Peter J. *Pacific Islanders Under German Rule: A Study in the Meaning of Colonial Resistance*, ANU Press, 1978. Pp 82-3

from time to time.[16] Cultists looking for Cthulhu's watery home would naturally be attracted to Ponape's Cyclopean masonry and the legend of how it came to be.

> According to Pohnpeian legend, Nan Madol was constructed by twin sorcerers Olisihpa and Olosohpa from the mythical Western Katau, or Kanamwayso. The brothers arrived in a large canoe seeking a place to build an altar so that they could worship Nahnisohn Sahpw, the god of agriculture. After several false starts, the two brothers successfully built an altar off Temwen Island, where they performed their rituals. In legend, these brothers levitated the huge stones with the aid of a flying dragon.[17]

Megalithic structures, twin sorcerers, flying dragon; what isn't there to attract a Cthulhu cultist? Pons

---

[16] The website "Beachcomber, Traders & Castaways in Micronesia" states, "Ever since foreign ships began visiting the islands, men came ashore to stay--some as deserters and beachcombers, some as castaways, some as traders. This is a list of those foreigners who came to Micronesia to stay--at least for a while. It includes foreigners who are proven to have lived ashore Palau, Yap, Chuuk, Pohnpei, Kosrae and the Marshalls during the 18th and 19th centuries." This is the link to Pohnpei (Ponape):
http://www.micsem.org/pubs/articles/historical/bcomber/pohnpei.htm
[17] Goran, David. "The Lost City of Nan Madol Is the Only Known Ancient City Ever Built on Top of a Coral Reef." *The Vintage News*, 14 Mar. 2016, https://www.thevintagenews.com/2016/03/15/lost-city-nan-madol-constructed-200-bc-archaeologists-no-idea-achived/.

probably filed away talk of and/or by worshippers of gods from the distant stars along with his other stores of knowledge. However, over the years, in the course of clipping news of crime from papers from every corner of the globe, he might have been struck by the similarities of cult activities in areas unconnected to one another. He might even had read of Inspector Legrasse's foray into the bayous. He would have detected a pattern and investigated on his own enough to write his monograph.

Why then the lie about the existence of the *Necronomicon* and the others when 6SIL saw print? Pons's monograph was probably a small-run publication intended for academics and law enforcement. Parker's adventure was intended for a mass audience, one in which the reality of the cult and associated books had long been blurred by Lovecraft and his acolytes. Pons may have seen no need to clear up the matter. Indeed, obscuration might be best for the world at large. Again, Pons's "archeological researches" were struck from BLKN[18] and mention of his two relevant dissertations on the matter never saw acknowledgment in Parker's adventures.

This article is agnostic on the existence of Cthulhu. As Pierre-Simon Laplace (1749- 1827) said, "The weight of evidence for an extraordinary claim must be proportioned to its strangeness." Nor does it draw any conclusions on Pons's view on the matter. "A healthy skepticism is a good attribute," said Pons in BLIN, "I like to keep an open mind. One can never be positive in matters of this kind, however rational it seems to deny

---

[18] Of course, that could be due to Pons's intelligence work on Ponape still being an official secret.

out of hand the manifestation of the so-called supernatural or extrasensory." He could certainly investigate a cult without believing the cult's tenets. If Pons did believe in the existence of Cthulhu that would certainly give more reason to forward the belief in its fiction hood.

Envoi

There is a strange coda to Pons's Ponapean perlustration. Governor Burg's untimely death on April 30, 1907 was noteworthy.

> Officially he died of sunstroke while out surveying—an unusual death for a man who had spent some nine years in the tropics. The Ponapeans themselves believe differently. Their oral traditions tell of Berg's digging in the ruins of Nan Madol and disturbing the tombs of the ancestral kings. He died a few days later, without any prior signs of illness, pursued to the end by the sound of ghostly shell trumpets echoing through the mountains. It is a tale of retribution entirely in keeping with the brooding atmosphere of Ponape and its people.[19]

Of course, a good story could use a bit of judicious editing and augmentation and a website like Historic Mysteries must figure a few juicy details couldn't hurt:

---

[19] Hempenstall p. 84

No written records on the island's history exist and it has been kept alive by oral tradition only. The local practice of keeping secrets is a sacred one. This was one of the obstacles to learning more about their history. The local king Nahmwarki made a proclamation saying to all, "To disrupt the holy ground that once belonged to past rulers with supernatural powers would be breaking the law." In fact, he threatened the English archeologist F.W. Christian with capital punishment should he break the law and dig. Jewelry and other artifacts that were buried with the chiefs were plundered... In 1874, a shipwreck near the Marshall Islands took hundreds of crates belonging to Polish anthropologist Jan Kubary, to the bottom of the ocean. With it went much of the island's history. In the early twentieth century, Germans governed the island when Governor Victor Berg dared to disregard the royal ban. He entered the sealed tomb on the island and opened the coffin of the ancient island rulers. In it he found the skeletal remains of giants measuring two to three meters tall.[20] That night, the island was

---

[20] Oceanic people are rather tall. Captain Cook, on his arrival in Hawaii met Chief Kaneena, who was describe as 6 feet (two meters)

alive with spirit activity. A wild storm came about with lightning flashes in the sky. Torrential rains pounded down on the island[21] as Governor Victor Berg lay in delirium, hearing the sounds of a conch shell blowing. The next morning, on April 30, 1907, Governor Berg died. The German physician serving on the island that night could not determine the cause of death, but the natives were certain that his death was a curse from the Gods for his blatant disrespect. Today's rationale says he died as a result of sunstroke and heat exhaustion contracted while surveying the ruins.[22]

The source Historic Mysteries offers no sources. Hempenstall's milder version, which states that Berg's digging in the ruins is part of local tradition, not fact, at least footnotes to his source, 1957's *The Eastern Carolines* by John L. Fischer with the assistance of Ann M. Fischer. And so unfounded rumor becomes legend. We can be sure that Pons would be more careful in his inquiries. And perhaps that is why the Cthulhu cult

---

tall, so a two meter skeleton would not be odd. "Two to three meters" leaves a lot of wiggle room.

[21] Ponape is one of the wettest places on earth, with an average of 188.0 inches of rain a year on the coast and 300.0 inches in some mountainous locations. No need to call on "spirit activity" for a storm on that night.

[22] Noa, Madeleine. "Nan Madol – Venice of the Pacific." *Historic Mysteries*, Historic Mysteries, 12 Oct. 2016, https://www.historicmysteries.com/nan-madol/.

receives no notice in Parker's chronicles except an oblique reference to certain minor American authors.

*****

Works Cited

Beachcombers, Traders & Castaways in Micronesia, http://www.micsem.org/pubs/articles/historical/bcomber/pohnpei.htm.

Carter, Lin. *Lovecraft: A Look Behind the "Cthulhu Mythos*. Ballantine Books, 1972.

Derleth, August. *The Dragnet Solar Pons*. Battered Silicon Dispatch Box, 2009.

German Colonies in the Pacific | National Library of Australia. https://www.nla.gov.au/selected-library-collections/german-colonies-in-the-pacific.

Goran, David. "The Lost City of Nan Madol Is the Only Known Ancient City Ever Built on Top of a Coral Reef." *The Vintage News*, 14 Mar. 2016, https://www.thevintagenews.com/2016/03/15/lost-city-nan-madol-constructed-200-bc-archaeologists-no-idea-achived/.

"H. P. Lovecraft Bibliography." *Wikipedia*, Wikimedia Foundation, 13 Dec. 2019, https://en.wikipedia.org/wiki/H._P._Lovecraft_bibliography.

J., Peter Hempenstall. *Pacific Islanders Under German Rule: A Study in the Meaning of Colonial Resistance*. ANU Press, 2016.

Lovecraft, Howard Phillips, and Leslie S. Klinger. *The New Annotated H.P. Lovecraft*. Liveright Publishing Corporation, 2014.

Noa, Madeleine. "Nan Madol – Venice of the Pacific." *Historic Mysteries*, Historic Mysteries, 12 Oct. 2016, https://www.historicmysteries.com/nan-madol/.

"Pohnpei." *Wikipedia*, Wikimedia Foundation, 20 Nov. 2019, https://en.wikipedia.org/wiki/Pohnpei.

*****

Biographical note about the author:

James C. O'Leary, a long-time Sherlockian and Ponsian, was made a member of the Praed Street Irregulars by Luther Norris. He is a contributor to the I Hear of Sherlock Everywhere website.

"The Name is Pons... *Solar* Pons!"

By Robert Pohle, PSI

Now, while there is no doubt that Solar Pons is not Sherlock Holmes, some of the other possible identifications in the Pontine Canon are less unambiguous.

For one example, let us look at the British secret agent Ashenten, who figures in the great Pons tale "The Adventure of the Orient Express." And I do mean let us *look* at him, for in the illustration on Page 19 of the original separate publication of this tale by The Candelight Press, [1] Ashenten has been drawn by the great Pontine illustrator Henry Lauritzen [2] to unmistakably resemble Franco-British author W. Somerset Maugham. [3]

Maugham, of course, *did* serve in the British Secret Intelligence Service: it was later to be rather well known as MI6 (if a secret organization could in fact properly be said to *be* "well known," at least without implying a criticism).

Recruited by a highly placed intelligence officer known as "R," Maugham eventually fictionalized some of his espionage experiences in his book of linked short stories *Ashenden: Or the British Agent* (1927). Delightful as these stories are, one can only wish that Winston Churchill had not advised Maugham to burn quite a few of what would have been additional stories about Ashenden. While they would have made the book much longer and no doubt even more delightful, one supposes that Churchill thought that perhaps they would not have been *quite* so delightful to "R".

Nevertheless, in subsequent years Maugham *did* in fact write and publish still more stories about Ashenden, including the tale "Sanatorium" in the anthology *Creatures of Circumstance* (1947). Three years later, Maugham brought "Sanatorium" to the screen in his film *Trio* (1950). One must note that *Trio* is not just adapted from Maugham stories, but is also one of the several films in which Maugham portrays *himself* on screen-- apparently because he was getting good and tired of Herbert Marshall portraying him. [4]

Is it entirely a coincidence that just three years after this, another former British agent named Ian Fleming published his book *Casino Royale* (1953)?

Now we enter into murkier waters. When Lauritzen drew "Ashenten" to resemble Maugham, was he telling us that "Ashenten" was in fact the same person as "Ashenden"? Admittedly, the difference of a single consonant would not seem to offer much of a disguise, but one supposes that spies have made do with even less transparent devices.

Now let us consider. Is Ashenten, Ashenden? Is Bond, Ashenten? Is Maugham Ashenten as well as Ashenden? Is Herbert Marshall, Maugham? Is Maugham, Maugham? The questions multiply in ascending and descending progressions like an M.C. Escher drawing.

When we first encounter Ashenten in "The Adventure of the Orient Express," he is described by Dr. Parker as "A slender Englishman, medium in build" -- but one must admit that he is portrayed by Henry

Lauritzen as neither very "slender" *nor* very "medium" in Lauritzen's accompanying illustration in the 1965 separate edition. [5] Stoutish, in fact.

[In view of the many ambiguities of identity which we are discussing, one might note that *our* Dr. Lyndon Parker is *not* the distinguished scientist Dr. Lyndon Ormond-Parker of Alyawarre descent, however much one might be gratified to find a connection.]

Returning to our story and *our* Dr. Parker: when he is describing the deceased Ashenten (Whoops! Too late for a Spoiler Alert?), Dr. Parker notes indeed that "The body was comparatively slight," but we must carefully consider these terms. Just what constitutes *comparative* slightness? Is a plump man slight compared to a portlier one? Is Oliver Hardy slight when compared to a whale?

More problems of identity arise. Baron Egon Von Ruber says that Ashenten "was unmarried, he leaves no family..." One must admit that although in 1938 when "The Adventure of the Orient Express" takes place, Maugham was indeed divorced and therefore single... still, Maugham was *not* childless. He had, in fact, a daughter (we will leave aside his none-too-gallant suspicions about her paternal parentage).

Of course, we are under no obligation to trust Von Ruber's words. If anything, we should tend to doubt them. Dr. Parker alludes to the Baron's evident "duplicity" more than once during the story... although the good doctor does not quite learn the full *extent* of that duplicity until the *denouement*.

In that same category of dubiety, we might put the Baron's claim about Ashenten that "there was bark in him still. I suspect somewhere there is a woman-- he was susceptible to them." Here we are in murkier waters. Maugham was indeed "susceptible" to ladies, especially in his earlier life, but by 1938 his susceptibilities had tended to focus more on gentlemen (and indeed on some who were less than gentlemanly). Might we add this ambiguity to the many ambiguities of identification in this story? And might one wonder just a bit about a possible connection to the ambiguities of The Agent August Derleth's own complexities in these matters? Not that Derleth is Parker, of course. Any more than Pons is Holmes.

We could go on. "The Adventure of the Orient Express" also features other memorable characters such as M. Hercule Poiret, who is apparently a Frenchman, *quite* unlike his Belgian colleague M. Poirot-- who was known to ride the Orient Express occasionally himself, in fact. But we will postpone our examination of the story's other delightful ambiguities until another essay.

[Full disclosure: the present author is inordinately proud of having been honored with the PSI investiture of "Ashenten." And, if there is indeed a bit of Ashenten in Bond... James Bond... then I find that I am unable to resist the temptation to mention as well the several books I wrote about (and with) the late Sir Christopher Lee, a close family relation of Ian Fleming's, and the portrayer of Fleming's title villain Scaramanga, both in the memorable Bond film *The Man with the Golden Gun* (1974) and also in the cover illustration of my *Christopher Lee Film Encyclopedia (2017)*.]

ENDNOTES:

[1] Derleth, August, 1965; *The Adventure of the Orient Express*. New York: Candlelight Press. My references are to the Second Printing, September 1965. In 1973 after the passing of The Agent, the story was posthumously gathered into *The Chronicles of Solar Pons*.

[2] The late lamented Henry Lauritzen was not only surely the finest Pontine illustrator but perhaps coincidentally also a classic artist of Sherlockian portraiture. One feels that there is indeed a certain resemblance between Holmes and Pons--at least as Lauritzen drew them, anyway.

[3] The immortal novelist/spy William Somerset Maugham (1874-1965).

It must be borne in mind that the Lauritzen illustration in the 1965 separate edition of *The Adventure of the Orient Express* is reproduced in a significantly larger size than it subsequently appears in *The Original Text Solar Pons Omnibus Edition* in 2000, so that the details are easier to see and the portraiture of Maugham as Ashenten consequently much more obvious. The fact that the 1965 publication has only 60 pages while the 2000 omnibus has over 1,200 pages, accounts for the roominess of the original illustrations, and the constrictions of the later ones!

[4] Herbert Brough Falcon Marshall (1890-1966) was indelibly memorable as the Maugham surrogate in the

movie of *The Moon and Sixpence* (1942), and most especially as the filmic incarnation of Maugham himself in *The Razor's Edge* (1946).

The actual mundane off-screen real-life Maugham was apparently increasingly displeased when people who met his own tangible self, were quite transparently disappointed that he did not much resemble the tall, suave and elegant Marshall. Among other details, Marshall's speaking voice-- universally acknowledged as one of the most beautiful voices in films-- contrasted noticeably with the real Maugham's lifelong speech impediment, about which he was always self-conscious.

Maugham, therefore, began to play the character of Maugham himself on screen in films like *Quartet* (1948), *Trio* (1950, featuring Ashenden) and *Encore* (1951). Sadly, although Maugham was now much more recognizable to filmgoers, they were still apparently a bit crestfallen that he did not resemble Marshall. Oh well.

[5] Again, it must be remembered how much more detail is visible in the 1965 original illustration than in the reduced reproduction in the 2000 *Omnibus*.

Biographical note about the author:

Robert Pohle, **PSI** has appeared in over 30 books, as contributor or sole author, and keeps saying that he is retired, apparently to no avail. He was honored to receive from the Lord Warden of the Pontine Marshes an investiture in the PSI as "Ashenten." Among Pohle's quasi-Pontine writings are his mystery/western crossover *Three Problems for Virgil Earp* (2011, Treble Heart Books) which was intended as a tip of the Stetson hat to The Agent's *Three Problems for Solar Pons* (1952)...and a copy of which is now almost as hard to find.

Did Solar Pons Really Meet Hercule Poirot on the Orient Express?

By Chris Chan

August Derleth's Solar Pons series contains many connections to the universes of other famous characters. The most prominent of these is Sherlock Holmes himself, who is referenced multiple times throughout the Pontine canon, and it is explicitly stated that Holmes and Pons have consulted together on some cases. The great defense attorney Perry Mason is name-checked in one story as a person existing in the same universe as Pons, as is the scientist, lawyer, and detective Dr. John Thorndyke. On multiple occasions, Pons interacts with a mysterious Chinese man who is implied to be Dr. Fu Manchu, and H.P. Lovecraft's Cthulhu universe is occasionally referenced.

Perhaps the Solar Pons story with the most inter-universe crossovers is "The Adventure of the Orient Express." Over the course of the story, Pons and Parker come across a series of characters who may be the adventurer Bulldog Drummond, Simon Templar (also known as The Saint), W. Somerset Maugham's "British Agent" Ashenden, and George Valentine Williams' Dr. Adolph Grundt (nicknamed "Clubfoot").

Notably, and probably for copyright reasons, none of these characters are identified by name. Of the aforementioned characters, one is identified only as having a face comparable to a bulldog, another character's clubfoot is emphasized; there is a reference to "Colonel Somerset," and one presumably undercover character signs a note with a stick figure sporting a halo. These are in-jokes for fans of the original characters, and if one is unfamiliar with the original characters, the references will probably pass over the readers' heads. The failure to use the actual names is deliberate, for Derleth did not have the rights to use the actual characters.

But there is one character who appears in "The Adventure of the Orient Express" who is explicitly named: Hercule Poiret. Many readers and critics have assumed that this is in fact Agatha Christie's legendary detective Hercule Poirot, with an accidental or deliberate "e" substituted for the second "o," but is this really the case? Why would Poirot/Poiret be the one character to make a cameo and be named? If the one-letter difference wasn't an accident, could it be deliberate?

Christie's Poirot certainly has a famous connection to the train featured in the Pons story. *Murder on the Orient Express* is definitely one of, if not *the* most well-known Hercule Poirot mysteries. It's not surprising that he should make an appearance... but if it were really meant to be Christie's Poirot, why is he named and not simply identified by his enormous waxed moustaches, and allowed to be a subtle in-joke reference like the other aforementioned characters? Simply by being named, and with the name wrongly spelled, it seems as if this isn't Christie's Poirot at all.

Additionally, the Poiret character simply does not *act* like Christie's Poirot. He identifies as a member of the French Sûreté, when anybody with even a rudimentary knowledge of Christie's Poirot knows that he is a proud Belgian with no connection to the French investigative forces. If Christie's Poirot were to go undercover as a French policeman, why would he use his own name, or something so close to it? Why claim to be a French officer of the law when at that time (the mid-1930's), the name of Hercule Poirot was famous throughout Europe? Furthermore, Poiret seems to move more nimbly than Poirot, who suffered from a nasty limp in his first appearance, though this disability was not mentioned in later novels, though he still had difficulty walking long distances. Worst of all, Poiret is not a very good detective– he is officious in manner, and easily fooled by Pons' subterfuge. The differences lead to one conclusion. Poiret is not Poirot.

So why would the character of Poiret be created? August Derleth is on record as being critical of Agatha Christie's legendary Poirot novel *The Murder of Roger Ackroyd*, arguing in his book *Writing Fiction* that the solution to that mystery was a cheat, a common opinion early in the twentieth century, though one that has been largely overshadowed today by the approving perspective voiced by Dorothy L. Sayers, which was "Fair! And fooled you!" Did Derleth's displeasure at one of Agatha Christie's greatest literary triumphs and twist endings lead him to take a little dig at her most famous creation? It is possible, though any thoughts on Derleth's motives must remain pure speculation.

Incidentally, the name "Poiret" would take on another meaning in the twenty-first century, long after Derleth's death. There has long been speculation that

Christie's character name may have been inspired by Marie Belloc Lowndes' Hercules Popeau, though this is a controversial suggestion, in the novel *The D Case: Or The Truth About The Mystery of Edwin Drood*, authors Carlo Fruttero and Franco Lucentini bring many famous detectives such as Sherlock Holmes, Father Brown, Nero Wolfe, and many more together to investigate the solution to Charles Dickens' unfinished novel. In it, Popeau claims that Poirot is derived from him, though other scholars disagree. The influential crime writer Martin Edwards notes that much of the theorizing about the origins of Poirot's name is unreliable, and that both Popeau and Poirot are unique characters.

But in recent years, many online sources have commented on the mysteries of Jules Poiret, which were supposedly written in the early twentieth century by Frank Howell Evans. Jules Poiret is a retired Belgian police officer living in London, who solves crimes with his friend Captain Howard (Christie's Poirot's best friend was Captain Hastings). The Jules Poiret mysteries are very similar to Christie's stories, and are widely proclaimed to be an inspiration for Christie's work. The twist is, the background of the Jules Poiret mysteries is a hoax. They were written far more recently, are a deliberate parody or pastiche of Christie's Poirot, and the claims that Christie was inspired by them (or even plagiarized them) are a tissue of lies. Jules Poiret is a twenty-first century creation, and many of his mystery titles are derived from Christie's original titles. The Jules Poiret mystery *Lord Hammershield Dies* is obviously taken from Christie's *Lord Edgware Dies*, *Murder on the Thames* comes from Christie's *Death on the Nile*, and *Murder on the Liverpool Express* needs no explanation.

In conclusion, the Hercule Poiret in "The Adventure of the Orient Express" is very likely *not* the Hercule Poirot of Agatha Christie, but instead is a parody or pastiche, or, if the name is in fact a pun on Derleth's part, a "pirate."

*****

Biographical note about the author:

Chris Chan is a writer and educator. He is a researcher and "International Goodwill Ambassador" for Agatha Christie Ltd., and writes for *Gilbert!* and *The Strand*. He is also the author of the Funderburke mystery series.

The Long Return of Solar Pons

By David Marcum, PSI

In 2017, my collection of thirteen Solar Pons stories, *The Papers of Solar Pons*, was published. It was the first collection of Pons stories authorized by the August Derleth Estate since those written by Basil Copper in the 1970's. The publication of that book led to the reappearance of all of the original Derleth Pons volumes in 2018, in new affordable editions – paperbacks, hardcovers, e-books, and audio versions – for a new generation. After that, 2019 saw *The Further Adventures of Solar Pons*, collecting twenty new Pons stories by a range of modern authors. And more is on the way.

The return of Pons might have happened anyway, but in this particular case, it can be traced back to an offhand suggestion by an elementary school librarian nearly half-a-century ago.

In the fall of 1973, August Derleth had been dead for a little over two years. During his lifetime, he wrote a vast number of books – historical fiction, poetry, science fiction, biographies, and mysteries. In wider circles, he is perhaps best remembered for his ambitious *Sac Prairie Saga*, telling the story of the area in which he was born, lived, and died, Sauk City, Wisconsin. He is also well known for his tireless efforts in preserving, promoting, and expanding the works of H.P. Lovecraft. But within

Sherlockian circles, he will always be remembered for bringing forth *Solar Pons*.

For Derleth, the Pons stories were a labor of love, but they weren't always well known. The first were initially written in the 1920's, and then the Ponsian Fields lay fallow until after World War II when, at the encouragement of Sherlockians Ellery Queen and Edgar W. Smith, Derleth began to revisit 7B Praed Street, pulling further adventures from Dr. Parker's Tin Dispatch Box. (And I'm certain that Parker also had one of those, just like Dr. Watson's.) Although some were published in various mystery magazines over the next few decades, most went straight into the Pons volumes that Derleth self-published – mostly new stories, as well as the occasional magazine reprints thrown into the collection. These books were known in Sherlockian circles, and occasionally collected in libraries, but for the most part Pons was someone who had to be sought rather than accidentally discovered. Luckily I accidentally discovered him, and I think that it changed my life.

When I was eight years old, in 1973, I first discovered the actual joy of reading, and what hooked me was a mystery story. One day in third grade, my class was in the library and the teacher told us that we had to check out a book. Now, I'd always had a love for books, and started reading very early. When I was five or six, my dad bought a giant set of shelves and, after he had assembled them, he brought down several boxes from our attic containing his own books from when he was a kid in the 1940's – volumes of Tarzan (my first "book friend", as my son later came to call them), and

Robinson Crusoe, and *Treasure Island*, and different Lone Ranger and Red Ryder books, and so many others – shelves and shelves of them, all given to me.

Soon after, he received an advertisement for a set of the complete works of Dickens, bound in some sort of greenish leather. He threw the flyer away, but I dug it out of the trash – showing great taste and intelligence for a six-year old – and timidly asked if he'd buy them. He gathered me up in his lap and asked why – as I knew nothing about Dickens except for probably having seen a cartoon version of *A Christmas Carol* – and I replied that I just thought that they looked good. So, he *did* buy them – even though I'm sure that we couldn't afford them – and then he did the same a few months later with a smaller set of Mark Twain novels. And I *did* read them, some several times, and the fact that he bought them for me without question is an amazing memory.

But that day in the elementary school library, with no idea as to what I should choose, I was getting a little desperate. Finally, the librarian pointed toward a row of low shelves and said that those were *mysteries*, and to try one. I have no idea who she was – I can't remember her name, or her age, or her face. She was a nice and probably harried elementary school librarian in a poor little East Tennessee school library in the early 1970's, but by pointing me toward that set of mysteries, she directed me through a magical door. I looked around, and finally a title jumped out at me. I grabbed it and checked it out, little realizing that it would change my life.

No, it wasn't a book about Pons. I doubt that his adventures were in many – or any – elementary school libraries in eastern Tennessee in the early 1970's. (They probably still aren't.) What I found was *The Mystery of the Green Ghost* by Robert Arthur (1909-1969), the fourth book in a relatively new – at that time – children's mystery series, *The Three Investigators*. It was the first mystery that I'd ever read, and there was no going back.

Reading that excellent series first led directly to Pons, and then indirectly to my great interest in the adventures of Mr. Sherlock Holmes. Partially the nature of the books themselves prepared me to enjoy those kinds of stories. The Three Investigators stories had perfectly linear mysteries with real clues. They were well-written, and I can (and do) still go back and enjoy them today – and I can't always say about The Hardy Boys books, which I found soon after. One of the gimmicks of The Three Investigators books was that the team of boy investigators, the leader of which was very Sherlockian in his manner of thinking, lived near Hollywood, and at the end of each book, they would visit with real-life film director Alfred Hitchcock at his studio and recount their latest case. In return, Hitchcock would then write an introduction to the latest book.

In actual fact, Hitchcock didn't write anything at all. Robert Arthur, the author, had a long professional relationship with Hitchcock, and had convinced the famous director to allow his presence to be included as a character in the book series, no doubt with some financial remuneration mixed in. By the time The Three Investigators books were first published in 1964, Robert Arthur had been an author for many years, writing short stories, and also scripts for radio and television. Additionally, he was a gifted behind-the-scenes editor, putting together the various mystery short story collections with Alfred Hitchcock's name on them. (You may have seen or read some of them.)

After creating The Three Investigators, Arthur went on to edit a series of oversized hardback mystery anthologies for children, again with Hitchcock's name on them, as if Hitchcock had edited them himself, but with an acknowledgement on the copyright page stating: *The editor gratefully acknowledges the invaluable assistance of Robert Arthur in the preparation of this volume.*

And now we come to how this off-trail discussion of The Three Investigators and those related Robert Arthur anthologies for children is relevant to Solar Pons. In the children's anthology *Alfred Hitchcock's Daring Detectives* (1969), which I read as a sort-of extension of The Three Investigators, Arthur included a Pons story, "The Adventure of the Grice-Paterson Curse" (De Waal 5624). Arthur, writing as Hitchcock, stated in the book's introduction:

> *And last, but not least, as a special treat I am including a detective who may seem oddly familiar to you, though the name is strange. Who exactly is Solar Pons, of "The Adventure of the Grice-Paterson Curse", and his companion, Dr. Parker? Surely they can't be – No, no, they are not the Great Detective and his medical friend in disguise.* (Arthur goes on to state that) *[t]hey are instead two characters created . . . to carry*

on a tradition known and loved by every reader of detective stories.

This story, which I read when I was eight years old, was truly my first introduction to the Holmes-Watson template, although I didn't realize it then. As any Pons enthusiast knows, it's an amazing story, and it's still my favorite Pons adventure to this day. And it made a deep impression on me.

I'm sure that memories of this story were still percolating in my subconscious when I picked up my first real Holmes book two years later. I had enjoyed everything about "The Grice-Paterson Curse" so much that when I started "The Red-Headed League", the first story in the 1955 Whitman abridged edition of *The Adventures* that I'd recently received (rather reluctantly) in a trade with a friend, I already had a familiarity for the form in my head, and Holmes and Watson found ready acceptance there.

So it turns out that I discovered Pons first, which isn't the way most people find their way to Holmes and Watson and Baker Street. That one story, "The Grice-Paterson Curse", was nothing more than a pleasant curiosity to me as I kept reading about Sherlock Holmes. I was a kid, and never thought about finding other Pons stories, and wouldn't have been able to if I'd tried. But then, a few years after Derleth's 1971 death, the Pons adventures were finally made available to the masses in the form of Pinnacle paperback editions. I saw those in a bookstore and recognized the Holmesian connection from Pons's representation on the cover – in deerstalker and Inverness. I asked for (and received) the entire

Pinnacle paperback set as a birthday gift from my parents, and then I kept going when Pinnacle began publishing the subsequent Basil Copper Pons pastiches as well. I continued to enjoy Pons as other materials appeared intermittently over the years – the Copper Omnibus (with his deplorable edits), the additional Copper pastiches from other publishers, and the rediscovered "lost" material brought forth by George Vanderburgh and The Battered Tin Dispatch Box.

During that time, the general public – even many Sherlockians – began to forget about Pons. Bob Byrne kept the flame burning with his blogs and newsletters and website, *www.solarpons.com*. He and I began to correspond, and I wrote a few essays for his newsletter. At some point, he suggested that he might devote an issue entirely to Pons pastiches. Since Pons was (and is) still owned by the Derleth Estate, the stories would have to be fan-fiction – which would work, as they would be published in the free online newsletter. But I have an aversion to ephemeral electronic versions of things. I want real objects. I want *books*. An idea was forming in my mind.

When Bob first made the suggestion to write a Pons pastiche, I sat down immediately and did so, producing "The Adventure of the Doctor's Box" within just a day or so. And it was so much fun that I wrote two more almost as quickly. I sent them to Bob, with the suggestion that he might ask around in Derleth circles to see if they could be included in an authorized real book that would sit on a shelf and exist into the future, rather than simply in an e-file that could vanish with a silent *blip*. (I've archived and printed on real paper hundreds and hundreds of traditional Sherlockian pastiches that have since vanished from the internet, so I know how easily this can happen.) After a while, when the pastiche newsletter wasn't happening, I decided to pursue the book idea myself.

I asked around and found out that the August Derleth Estate now consists of his grandchildren, Danielle Hackett and Damon Derleth. I obtained Danielle's email address and wrote to her – out of the blue – on August 21st, 2016, introducing myself, explaining my passion for Pons, and asking if it might be possible to publish an authorized collection of new Pons stories, in the same way that Basil Copper had done in the 1970's. I made the case that, with my contacts and growing experience in the Sherlockian community in relation to Holmes books that I'd written and edited, and with the new modern publishing paradigm and social media, a new awareness of Pons could be achieved, possibly wider than he'd originally had in past decades. Amazingly, Danielle agreed, replying within just a few days that she'd be happy to hear more details. We exchanged further emails, and the idea began to become a reality.

At that point, I reached out and explained the idea to my friend, Derrick Belanger, who had recently started Belanger Books with his brother, Brian. He was interested and introduced himself to Danielle, addressing the publishing end of the matter. In the meantime, I set about writing more Pons adventures – enough to make a full book.

I'm not sure how many that I initially thought would be enough, but as I started writing, the muse (in the form of Dr. Lyndon Parker) kept speaking, and I ended up with twelve new adventures. Like "The Doctor's Box", many have a connection with Sherlock Holmes – either dealing with later events related to a past Canonical case, or crossing Holmes's trail in London or Dartmoor. And of course, several were uniquely Pons's adventures, without the shadow of Holmes in the background. As a bonus, I included a story, "The Other Brother", written several years before as the finale of my first book, *The Papers of Sherlock Holmes*, detailing an origin story for Pons, and relating his connection to the Holmes family.

The Papers of Solar Pons was published in 2017, and hopefully caused a reawakening of interest in Pons. At about the same time, the Copper pastiches were also collected and reissued by PS Publishing, although they sadly gave the implied impression that the Copper editions were *The Complete Solar Pons*, without adequately acknowledging that Derleth created Pons and wrote over seventy of his adventures first.

Naturally, as my book and the Copper reissues appeared, people wondered about how to find and read the original Pons adventures. Thus, the next logical step was to reissue the originals to a new generation. Danielle and the Derleth Estate were willing, as was Belanger Books. So, the next phase began – a long and lonesome solitary exercise on my part that turned into a much bigger bite than I'd intended to chew. But it was worth it.

By this point – 2018 – the original Pons books published by Derleth's imprint, Mycroft and Moran, were very expensive collectibles, and even the Pinnacle

Paperbacks from the 1970's had become rare and costly. Most people who had heard of Pons couldn't afford to read about him. When it was announced that the original Pons books would be reissued, there was a growing wave of excitement. But first they actually had to be produced.

I own all the versions of the Pons books – the original Mycroft and Moran editions, the Pinnacle paperbacks, the Copper and Battered Silicon Dispatch Box omnibi, the British editions – a gift from my friend, Sherlockian and Ponsian Roger Johnson – and a few others besides. I quickly realized that the originals were the best source material, so I began scanning the Mycroft and Moran editions into electronic files – one page at a time, story after story, book after book, hour after hour after tedious hour. Then, when I finally had them all scanned, I took those files and used a text conversion software to turn them into a Word document. But that wasn't anywhere near the end of the process, for those scans were nowhere near readable.

The next step was cleaning all of that mess up. Text conversion is not pretty, or accurate, or correct. For instance, as seen in most older books, before text was automatically adjusted by writing software, words at the end of line were often broken up by hyphens. It was that way in the original Pons volumes. I had to go through and un-hyphenate thousands and thousands of words, along with simply laying out the text into proper paragraphs, with the correct spacing and punctuation.

Once that process was complete, I then had to read each of the stories – which was truly a pleasure – looking for all the things that the conversion and initial general formatting had missed. Often this involved line-by-line comparisons with the original volumes. Through much of 2018, in addition to real life and family and work, as well as writing Sherlock Holmes stories and editing multiple Holmes anthologies, I was chipping away at the Pontine Canon, story by story by story. I recall reading and editing them in all sorts of locations – at the free hotel breakfast while at an out-of-town work conference, or during my lunch hour every day, or on Sunday mornings while eating a bagel.

After I would finish a volume, having gone through the whole scan-and-convert process, and then the many subsequent hours of clean-up and editing, I would send the files to Derrick and Brian Belanger, who then gave it another read-through, checking for what I had missed. They caught things that I should have seen, and they also questioned odd things that – when compared to the original Mycroft and Moran editions – had to stay after all, as that's the way that Derleth originally wrote it – sometimes inexplicably.

(I was amazed as I read the original stories with a fresh and editorial eye at just how many changes Basil Copper had made when he prepared his 1982 *Omnibus* edition. Not only had he altered many of Derleth's Americanisms and spellings, to the anger of purists at the time of its publication, but I also found that he had changed whole dates in the text – sometimes refashioning a digit to move a story into a different *decade!* – and he even left out entire lines in order to make the stories fit into his own chronological arrangement. I knew that Pons scholars had long criticized his efforts – which was ironic because Copper later became quite hostile when people changed *his* Pons stories – but I had no idea until I dug into the originals just how much Copper had transformed.)

There are six original volumes of Pons short stories, and one novel. Additionally, there is enough apocryphal material to fill an eighth volume with essays and adventures as well as a second novel. By the middle of 2018, the first four books of short stories were ready and published, to great excitement. Brian Belanger, who had created a stunning and unforgettable cover for my own Pons collection, *The Papers of Solar Pons*, came up with covers in a similar style for the reissues of the originals. Just as the Mycroft and Moran editions had their own distinctive look, and then the Pinnacle paperbacks were unforgettable with their Robert Fawcett cover paintings, Brian's covers make this set something that collectors and fans will be proud to own.

I steadily continued the editing of the rest of the original Pons books through 2018, sending them to Derrick and Brian, and the remaining four volumes – the rest of the short stories, the novels, and the Apocrypha – were published at the end of that year. It was an amazing experience, and I wouldn't trade it, in spite of all the hours involved. But it wasn't over.

In 2019, I was able to assemble and edit *The Further Adventures of Solar Pons*, with twenty new adventures. This was the first time that multiple authors had been authorized to visit 7B Praed Street and bring back their own new stories. I wrote two more stories for this collection, proving to myself that my own efforts at writing Pons weren't finished. Now the original tales are slowly making their way into audio versions, and another volume of new Pons stories is in preparation as I write this, this time with Lovecraft-related narratives. Another, featuring Pons and Holmes stories, is planned after that, and maybe another collection by multiple authors. I've already written a Pons story for the Lovecraft collection, and – if I can find the time – I have ideas and plans for another full Pons collection of my own.

I have such great affection for Solar Pons and Dr. Parker. The stories are amazing in their own right, and they build so well upon the world of Sherlock Holmes. But more than that, I have to recall how I first ended up reading a mystery story that day in 1973, when I could have so easily ended up reading something that bored me and failed to ignite my imagination. I would have always eventually found and loved reading, and likely I would have discovered mysteries, but it might have occurred a totally different way, and down a totally different path. (God help me, I might have read and collected cat-cozies.) Thankfully, that anonymous elementary school librarian, whomever she was, took a couple of seconds to direct a dithering eight-year-old toward a particular shelf. And it's quite possible that because of her, Solar Pons has returned.

*****

Biographical note about the author:

David Marcum plays The Game with deadly seriousness. He first discovered Sherlock Holmes in 1975 at the age of ten, and since that time, he has collected, read, and chronologicized literally thousands of traditional Holmes pastiches in the form of novels, short stories, radio and television episodes, movies and scripts, comics, fan-fiction, and unpublished manuscripts. He is the author of nearly sixty Sherlockian pastiches, some published in anthologies and others collected in his own books, *The Papers of Sherlock Holmes*, *Sherlock Holmes and A Quantity of Debt*, and *Sherlock Holmes – Tangled Skeins*. He has edited nearly fifty books, many of them Sherlockian anthologies, including the ongoing series *The MX Book of New Sherlock Holmes Stories*, which he created in 2015. This collection is now up to 18 volumes, with several more in preparation. He was responsible for bringing back August Derleth's Solar Pons for a new generation, first with his collection of authorized Pons stories, *The Papers of Solar Pons*, and then by editing the reissued authorized versions of the original Pons books. He is now doing the same for the adventures of Dr. Thorndyke. He has contributed numerous essays to various publications, and is a member of a number of Sherlockian groups and Scions. He is a licensed Civil Engineer, living in Tennessee with his wife and son. His irregular Sherlockian blog, *A Seventeen Step Program*, addresses various topics related to his favorite book friends (as his son used to call them when he was small), and can be found at *http://17stepprogram.blogspot.com/* Since the age of nineteen, he has worn a deerstalker as his regular-and-only hat from autumn to spring, and often summer as well. In 2013, he and his deerstalker were finally able make his first trip-of-a-lifetime Holmes Pilgrimage to England, with return Pilgrimages in 2015 and 2016, where you may have spotted him. If you ever run into him and his deerstalker out and about, feel free to say hello!

To Pastiche or not to Pastiche

By Stephen Herczeg

As an author of both Sherlock Holmes and Solar Pons stories I'm often questioned about my writing. Understandably, many people know of Holmes but when Solar Pons is mentioned I'm generally greeted by blank stares. The expected change of expression, when I explain that Pons is a pastiche of Holmes, seldom comes, and I find myself launching into an elucidation of what constitutes a pastiche or at least what it means in terms of Solar Pons.

From an Australian point of view, I generally have to head off the unavoidable accusation that Pons is simply a *rip-off* of Holmes.

To aficionados the background behind the creation of Solar Pons is fairly well known, but it also helps to explain to laymen why August Derleth created the character in the first place. Generally, I tell people that Pons is an homage to Holmes as a way of celebrating the great detective and extending his tales into another time.

The next question is always, so Pons is a *send-up* of Holmes?

Australia is a country whose populace is imbued with a richly laconic sense of humour. Our comedians have generally been the type to take the piss out of our politicians and celebrities. Our greatest comedians, like Paul Hogan, Barry Humphries, and even Eric Bana (yes, the Hulk was once a comedian and a damned good one too), have used parodies of known celebrities and everyday Australians to great effect over the years. Numerous TV shows, such as *The Comedy Company*, *Fast Forward*, *The Gillies Report*, and any number of late-night talk shows, engage in the same act of parody to elicit laughs and to some respect point out the foibles of modern celebrities and politicians.

The United Kingdom and the United States are similarly infused with comedians and television shows of a similar ilk. From *Monty Python's Flying Circus*, *Not the Nine O'clock News,* and more recently *The Fast Show* in the UK, with the US leading the way for decades with *Saturday Night Live*.

Parody is seen as an exaggeration of a particular person or style to produce a comedic effect. Whereas, pastiche has always been a dedicated imitation of a style, work or person in a reverential style that effects a respectful homage to the original.

Whereas parody is generally created to elicit humour and can, in some cases, be disrespectful and downright deceitful in its interpretation, pastiche is meant to honour the original creator of the work in the sincerest form of adulation.

When Sir Arthur Conan Doyle set out and wrote his first Sherlock Holmes story, *A Study in Scarlet*, in 1887 he probably hoped beyond hope that his tale would be attractive to a small group of readers and would never have imagined the torrent of interest that his character would receive over the next 130 years.

Surprisingly, even the very first Holmes story triggered off what has become an industry in itself, the practice of writing parodies or pastiches of Sherlock Holmes.

The very first pastiche, as listed in *Sherlock Holmes Victorian Parodies and Pastiches: 1888-1899*, by Bill Peschel (2015), was called *Hampshire on Stilts*, under the pseudonym Donan Coyle in 1888. Though it could be called more of a pastiche of Arthur Conan Doyle rather than of his most admired character.

However, the first actual pastiche of Holmes, *My Evening with Sherlock Holmes*, was written in 1891 anonymously by J. M. Barrie of Peter Pan fame. It appeared in *Speaker* magazine in November 1891, a few months after the first Holmes short story *A Scandal in Bohemia* was published. It is interesting to note that a couple of months later Conan Doyle finally met and spent the evening in J. M. Barrie's company.

The Arthur Conan Doyle Encyclopedia website lists almost 300 individual pastiches and parodies of Sherlock Holmes published between 1888 and 1965. Some of the more notable names listed, as authors, are P. G. Wodehouse (several times), Mark Twain, and even John Lennon. The list also includes Sir Arthur Conan Doyle himself, as he wrote several Holmes-like stories as part of the evolution of his own detective. His son Adrian is also listed as having written about twelve new Holmes stories as well.

The list of pastiches post 1965 is possibly so expansive that the authors of the ACD Encyclopedia didn't have the resources available to track them all down.

We've also seen a continuous cavalcade of pastiches and parodies of Holmes in TV and Movies. I would be so bold as to suggest that all realisations of Sherlock Holmes in visual format are pastiches as they were not necessarily directly from the pen of Conan Doyle and have undergone some form of interpretation.

From the earliest known Holmes movie, *The Adventures of Sherlock Holmes* (1905), through to the abhorrent *Holmes & Watson* (2018), the character of Sherlock Holmes has appeared in well over three hundred movies and TV shows.

These examples are proof that there is an undying thirst for more stories and adventures involving the most famous detective of all time. There are crossovers with H. G. Wells, Steampunk, Edgar Allan Poe and other genres and sub-genres.

The popularity of the volumes of *The MX Book of New Sherlock Holmes Stories* from MX Press as well as the Sherlock Holmes anthologies from Belanger Books is evidence that the hunger will not die out any time soon.

In the midst of all the popularity of Holmes comes the existence of a Solar Pons. An honourable pastiche and homage to Holmes, using the basic elements of the Holmesian tales and characters to create a new overlapping universe set thirty to forty years in the future, with ties back to the original stories.

As mentioned, Pons's creator August Derleth approached Sir Arthur Conan Doyle to ask for permission to create new tales for Sherlock Holmes, but was met with a polite decline. One wonders whether all the other authors who had created pastiches up until that moment and from then on, approached Doyle in the same way or just continued on regardless.

Derleth took it upon himself to create a new detective with a slew of supporting characters and set the adventures nearer to his own time. The first volume of tales *In Re: Sherlock Holmes – The Adventures of Solar Pons* was released in 1945, well after Conan Doyle's death.

The world of Solar Pons brought with it a new level of technological improvements and over time began to overlap with a multitude of other authors' works, including H. P. Lovecraft, a close friend of Derleth's, Sax Rohmer (creator of Fu Manchu), W. Somerset Maugham (creator of Ashenden), and even the inclusion of characters based on Hercule Poirot and The Saint.

Although, Solar Pons is a much lesser known equivalent to Holmes, there is still a steady and very active fan base eager for new tales to slake their thirst.

So, from a writer's perspective, what is the attraction of writing pastiches of either Sherlock Holmes or Solar Pons?

Firstly, fun.

I have so far written six Sherlock Holmes stories and three Solar Pons stories, most of which have been accepted and published by Belanger Books. I have also worked with my daughter on a story that appeared in the young adult anthology *The Irregular Adventures of Sherlock Holmes*.

From a writer's perspective, the challenge of writing in the style of a Holmes/Pons story is an absolute delight, plus the added level of struggle that assaults the mind as the various strands of the story must be teased out and then woven back together to create a coherent ending is an incredibly enjoyable journey.

Couple that with the effusive reception that a new Holmes/Pons story receives amongst the aficionados and it presents as an almost addictive activity.

Secondly, humbling.

As stated, the welcome response that I have received from my stories, from both the editors and the public is an incredibly humbling experience.

Writers are a strange beast and generally inhabit their own minds for the majority of time. They also suffer from the continuous presence of imposter syndrome, whereby they sit in their dark, silent study, pounding away at the keyboard, waiting for the moment when someone will tap them on the shoulder and tell them they really aren't any good at what they do. We are filled with self-doubt and it is only a small percentage that ever gain enough confidence to submit our prose for consideration and an even smaller percentage that find their way into print.

Even, George R. R. Martin, creator of one of the most widely praised and accepted fantasy series of the last twenty years, has admitted that at times he ponders whether he is any good at what he does.

To create something that finds its way into print in the first place, and then finds a thankful audience fills the soul with joy and makes an author more confident to continue and create more stories.

Lastly, pride.

On the back of the humbling experience of creating a new Holmes or Pons story and finding acceptance amongst the Holmesian/Ponsian public, there is an ever-lasting sense of pride of a job well done.

That pride is the other driving force that can lift an author up and engender in them a desire to create more and more stories.

It is also a pride in the knowledge that there are others of the same ilk who possess similar aspirations and work to conceive and write stories that join with your own to share with a new generation of readers the joy and knowledge of well written detective stories in a style from almost a century ago.

In conclusion, I can say that from a personal perspective I thoroughly enjoy and indeed relish the prospect of writing pastiches of both Holmes and Pons, and plan to continue to do so well into the future.

In fact, quickly viewing the spreadsheet I keep for tracking upcoming submission deadlines, I see that I have five new pastiches to plot out and write, including a number of crossovers. If all goes well, most of them will find their way into print which spurs on my mind and hunger to no end.

*****

Biographical note about the author:

Stephen Herczeg is an IT Geek, writer, actor and film maker based in Canberra Australia. He has been writing for over twenty years and has completed a couple of dodgy novels, sixteen feature length screenplays and numerous short stories and scripts.

Stephen's scripts, *TITAN, Dark are the Woods, Control* and *Death Spores* have found success in the *International Horror Hotel, Horror Screenplay* and *Search for New Blood* screenwriting competitions with a win, a couple of runner-up and top ten finishes and a quarter finalist appearance.

His work has featured in *Sproutlings – A compendium of little fictions* from Hunter Anthologies, the *Hells Bells* Christmas horror anthology published by the Australasian Horror Writers Association and the *Below the Stairs, Trickster's Treats #1 and #2, Shades of Santa, Behind the Mask* and *Beyond the Infinite* anthologies from OzHorror.Con; *The Body Horror Book, Anemone Enemy* and *Petrified Punks* from Oscillate Wildly Press and *Beginnings*, from the Australian Speculative Fiction Group. He has had Sherlock Holmes stories published in *Sherlock Holmes in the realms of H.G. Wells, Sherlock Holmes: Adventures beyond the Canon* and *The MX Book of New Sherlock Holmes stories: Part XI* from Belanger Books.

Biographical note about the illustrator:

Brian Belanger, PSI is a Sherlockian publisher, editor, illustrator, cover designer and now (with this volume), poet. His cover designs can be seen on most Belanger Books and MX Publishing titles. With his brother, author Derrick Belanger, and author David Marcum, he helped restore August Derleth's original Solar Pons stories and currently publishes new adventures of the classic pulp detective. Brian lives in Manchester NH and is gearing up for a very busy 2020. Find his work at www.redbubble.com/people/zhahadun and https://zhahadun.wixsite.com/221b.

The Original Solar Pons Adventures

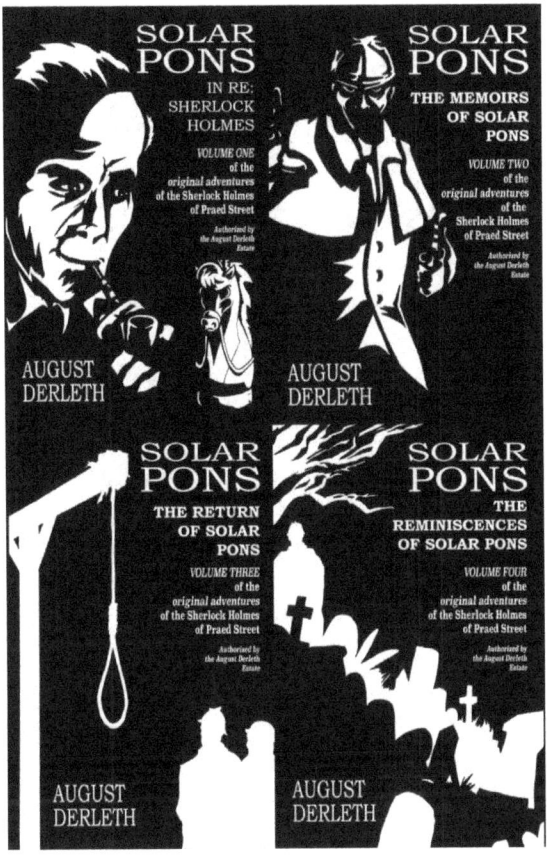

All seven original classics by August Derleth PLUS a volume of previously uncollected work. Available in beautiful new editions from Belanger Books!

The Papers of Solar Pons

The August Derleth Estate, Arkham House, and Belanger Books are pleased to present this authorized collection of twelve new Pons adventures by Sherlockian author and editor David Marcum. Join Pons and Parker as they venture forth into the mysterious London fogs during that murky period between the two World Wars. Along the way, meet some old friends, and discover why Pons is called "The Sherlock Holmes of Praed Street".

The New Adventures of Solar Pons

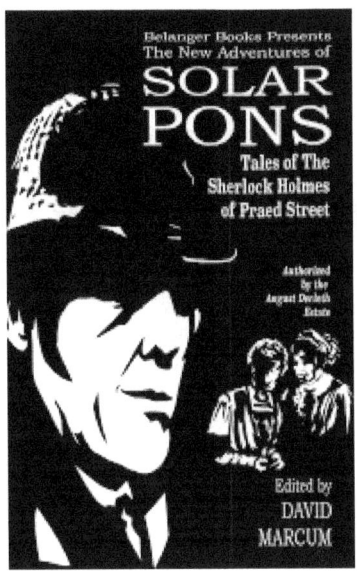

The estate of August Derleth has authorized the first ever anthology of Solar Pons stories! These twenty new adventures from Belanger Books range from soon after Pons and Parker met in 1919 to a story that occurs after Germany has been defeated in World War II. Each of them fully and traditionally falls within the Pontine Canon.

Belanger Books